CENTAURIA
THE ANCIENT REALM

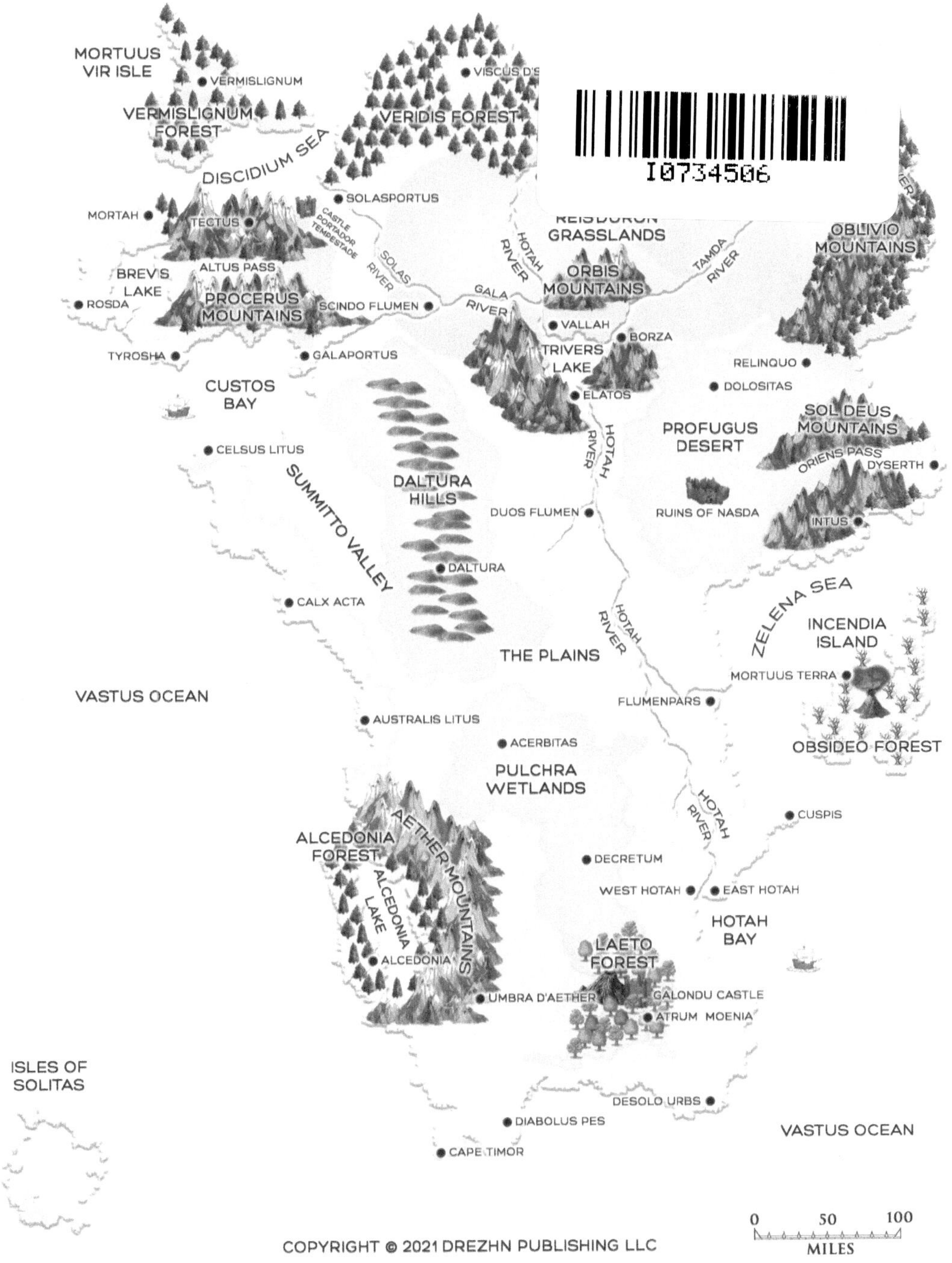

COPYRIGHT © 2021 DREZHN PUBLISHING LLC

SCOURGE

A WORLD OF CENTAURIA NOVELLA

DREZHN

PUBLISHING

SCOURGE

Published by Drezhn Publishing LLC
PO BOX 67458
Albuquerque, NM 87193-7458

Print Edition - June 2023
Version 1.8

Cover design by Drezhn Publishing LLC
Cover illustration by Jonathan Myers

HARDBACK (DUST JACKET) ISBN: 978-1-947328-19-8
HARDBACK (CASE LAMINATE) ISBN: 978-1-947328-74-7
PAPERBACK ISBN: 978-1-947328-14-3

BOOKS BY DANIEL KUHNLEY

EPIC DRAGON FANTASY

<u>The Dark Heart Chronicles</u>
*†The Dragon's Stone
*Reborn
*Rended Souls
True Heir

Scourge (novella)

SUPERNATURAL SERIAL KILLER

<u>Alice Bergman Novels</u>
*Birth Of A Killer (novella)
*The Braille Killer
*The Night Mauler
*The Chrono Slasher

CHRISTIAN YA SCI-FI/FANTASY
(as Daniel Luke Kuhnley)

<u>VR Academy</u>
Kiara Kole And The Key Of Truth

* - Also available as an audiobook
† - Previously released as Dark Lament

Visit Daniel's website to find these books and more!
danielkuhnley.com

First off, I'd like to thank my wife and best friend, Marsha, for helping me get the story outlined and fleshed out. Also, thanks go to her for updating the Ancient Realm map for this story that takes place over 1200 years before the events of *The Dark Heart Chronicles*.

Geoff, Phylls and Ryan, thank you for providing invaluable feedback that helped shape *Scourge* into an even better story.

I dedicate this book to those of you who have supported me over the years and continue to do so—fans both old and new alike. I wouldn't be doing this without you.

Last, but never least, all glory goes to Jesus Christ, my Lord and Savior.

Thank you all so much!

SCOURGE

A WORLD OF CENTAURIA NOVELLA

DANIEL KUHNLEY

Emorith Darkridge stood alone in the center of the granite slab road, her eyes wet with moisture, but far too little to satiate the fire within them. With her legs spread shoulder-width and her hands wrapped tight around her twisted staff, she leaned forward and craned her head back as far as it would go.

Two thousand feet above her, suspended just below the jagged, dome-shaped ceiling, hung the aethershard crystal.

The Äfäralleẕinzh.

Its dim light, born of a magical energy known in the world as mezhik, bathed the entire city in a bluish hue, a beacon to battle the forever-night of Intus.

She'd heard tales of its majesty and striking beauty, but all those accounts paled in comparison. The veins in her neck bulged and twitched as her pulse rose. She closed her eyes, yet its glow still filled her vision. Her skin pricked and the hairs on her nape and arms stood on end as its mezhik called to her.

She rose onto her tippy toes, stretched her arm up as far as she could reach, and willed its mezhik to consume her. Her toes departed from the ground, and she sailed into the air. Upward. So close to the ceiling, she felt its presence just above her head. She opened her eyes with a gasp, yet found her feet still rooted to the stone road and the crystal impossibly far from her grasp.

Her heart thrashed against her ribcage, jerking her forward with each beat. Beads of sweat lined her hairline and moistened her armpits. She rubbed her arms, but the chill remained.

Emorith breathed deep and realized her scarf had slipped down under her chin. An earthy, musty, rotten egg stench filled her nostrils and set her lungs afire.

The forges of Intus.

Her nose wrinkled. How anyone would choose to live beneath a mountain bewildered her, but the dwellers—a hairless, albino-skinned race of short-statured, humanoid creatures—flourished. Their hidden city spanned many square miles and boasted a palace hewn from solid stone and fit for the gods.

The dwellers of Intus did little trading with the outside world. In fact, few even knew of their existence. They would've faded from the memories of all Centauria long ago if not for their skilled craftsmanship with precious gems and metals. Their war hammers, maces, shields, and other forged weapons and armor rivaled that of the elves and their kinsman, the derro dwarves. However, unlike the fierce derro warriors, the dwellers fashioned themselves as arms dealers, willing to sell their goods to anyone for a price. Wars raged across Centauria through the ages, and kings and queens rose and fell from power, but the dwellers kept to their subterranean city under the mountain. Their haven.

Emorith's eyes narrowed.

Soon, they'll all be dead.

She knew none of them, yet the thought of taking part in wiping out an entire race unsettled her. Her stomach gurgled, and her chest ached right about where her heart should be, but she no longer had one. What must be done required her to feel nothing, and she told herself that she didn't, but her body failed to heed the commands of her mind.

She had to be strong. *Must* be strong. If not for herself, then for Illian.

Illian.

His name touched her heart like no other.

Flesh of my flesh.

Her first and only born. The others had been lost in her womb, spared from this harsh world by nameless gods.

Her hands trembled as tears welled in her eyes and her throat tightened. She ground her teeth and gripped her staff so hard that her knuckles turned white, and her hands ached. The tears receded, but her throat remained constricted.

Just find a test subject and be done with it.

Emorith dug her fingers into the leather pouch that hung from her waist, retrieved a wad of mint leaves, and stuffed them inside her left cheek. Succulent, refreshing juices seeped from the leaves as she worked a few of them between her back molars. The taste calmed her nerves.

She adjusted her scarf so that it covered her nose and mouth once again, but the thick air clung to the fabric and saturated the tightly woven strands of black silk. She pursed her lips.

Focus on the task and Magus will reward you.

She took pride in her persuasive mezhik skills, but she'd never believe her own lies. Magus Carac cared nothing for her—for anyone for that matter. He reigned over the southern half of the Ancient Realm with a bloody fist. No, the only reward she'd obtain from him would be an escape from punishment.

Magus sought ultimate power—to rule all Centauria, not just the southern half of the Ancient Realm. Like many of those under his strict rule, he used her time and again. Mentally. Physically. Magically. *Sexually.* She hated him for everything he did to her, but the arrival of Illian nine years ago made the steep price bearable.

Each task she performed for him darkened her soul further. Soon, she'd be lost forever, a shell of a woman without heart or soul. But she'd endure anything as long as Illian remained unharmed.

But will Magus keep his word?

She sighed, knowing she had no recourse if he didn't. No alternative existed that she could think of either. A man indifferent to his own flesh and blood could not be bargained or reasoned with. A tyrant. A mad king. War loomed on the horizon, and she must do his bidding once again.

Everything she'd done for Magus over the past ten years boiled down to this moment, and the only way she'd survive the night would be to do the unthinkable. She must locate a test subject and lure them to Magus with her powers of persuasion. Anything short of completing her task would earn her and Illian a one-way trip to Ef Demd Dhä, the realm of the damned, and bring them face-to-face with the dark one, DiƧäfär.

The thought made her skin crawl. She didn't bow down to DiƧäfär, nor did she serve Ƨäṭūr, the supposed "one true God." Her loyalties lie only with Illian. For him, she'd cross the veil of death and face any god or demon.

Illian's soft, green eyes, pale complexion, and thick raven hair drifted into her mind and tightened her throat. A single tear formed in the corner of her left eye. She wiped it away with the back of her hand.

I'll save you from your father, my love.

Had Emorith been one of the ʊnzhifṭäd, a person or creature born without mezhik, as Magus claimed Illian to be, Magus would've killed them both long ago. Twice, Magus had left her on the brink of death, and once, she'd crossed over into death before his vile mezhik ripped her back into the world. Never had she endured such agony. She never wanted to feel it again.

She stared at her hand and the thick scar across her palm. Her other palm had a matching scar of its own.

"A lesson in mind over matter," Magus had said, time and again.

How many times had he forced her to hold that length of glowing steel he'd pulled straight from the fiery forge? She couldn't recall, but her fingers curled, and her hand recoiled with the memory as pain seared her palm anew.

I'm stronger than this.

She took a deep breath and forced her gaze to the inside of her left wrist. A dark-blue, heart-shaped mark about an inch wide and tall marred her pale, freckled skin. On their sixteenth name day, each mage, wizard, and sorceress would gain their mezhik and their wizard's mark. Her heart-shaped mark symbolized the type of sorceress she'd become: Fizärd ImōƧzhn. As an emotion wizard, she possessed the power to release emotions that blocked true memories, an ability to gain knowledge of one's past based on reading emotions, and the gift of persuasion.

As with all wizards and sorceresses, Emorith possessed basic mezhik abilities beyond her classification as Fizärd Imōzhn. Some of those abilities, like conjuring balls of light or fire, telepathy, and telekinesis of small objects, required little effort and mezhik. Other abilities, like teleportation and basic healing, consumed far more mezhik based on the distance of teleportation or the severity of a wound. Expending too much mezhik, especially in the case of teleportation, could kill the wizard or sorceress.

With a single thought, an orange glow of mezhik—a white-hot heat that bubbled up from deep within the marrow of her bones—rose from her palm. Intense, yet soothing. She closed her palm and snuffed out the ball of light.

She closed her eyes and drifted into the past. She'd just turned eighteen the week prior to meeting Magus. She worked nights at the Drunken Fool's Tavern as a bar wench and had a reputation for garnering large tips. Drunken patrons and a touch of mezhik persuasion proved a perfect combination. No one knew her secret, and she split the extra coins with the other girls, so none of them ever questioned her or complained.

Magus came alone that night. His slicked-back, silver hair and piercing, yellow eyes grabbed her attention the moment he stepped through the door. His gaze scanned the patrons as he strode toward the bar—toward her. His eyes met hers, and his smile drew her in. Had she known then what she knew now, she never would've used her mezhik on him. Magus placed his hands on the counter and asked for a cup of water, but no one ordered water from her.

She smiled as she brushed her hand against his. Mezhik rose from within her, coating her tongue and lacing her words with persuasion. *"Are you sure you don't want a tankard of ale?"* she'd asked.

Magus's eyes narrowed and then the edges of his lips curled upward. He grabbed her left hand, quick as a snake's strike, and turned it over. He pushed up her sleeve before she could take a breath. She gasped.

He lowered her sleeve, turned her hand over, and kissed the top of it. He smiled, a devious glint in his eye. *"You're the one I've been looking for."*

Emorith pulled her hand back and rubbed her wrist. Her heart thundered.

She could no longer meet his steady gaze, so she stared at the napkin sitting on the bar between them. *"I am?"*

"Emotion is a rare gift," Magus had said. *"Your talents are wasted collecting coins from drunkards. Join me, and we can reshape the world into a better place. A place where you'll never have to hide who you are. It's time you shared your gift with the world."*

She breathed deep and opened her eyes. Intus bloomed into view once again, but its details blurred with tears.

Gifted... to what end?

With Magus, only one path existed.

Slavery.

Emorith balled her hand into a fist and gritted her teeth. "This is the last thing I do for you, Magus."

She ground the wad of mint leaves between her molars, working her jaws to squeeze the succulent juices from them, but their taste diminished with each passing moment. Soon, the fresh taste morphed into a putrid amalgamation of mint and sulfur.

She lowered her scarf and spat the wad out. The half-inch ball sailed several feet before crashing onto the solid surface and scuttling across it for several more. She looked about, but the road remained empty and the buildings dark.

Her brow furrowed as she turned her attention back to the wad. She glared at it and pointed a long, slender finger at it. *"Diẑinṭäzhräiṭ."*

The wad of blackened mint leaves burst with orange flames, turned to ash, and sank into a narrow fissure between the stones. She'd give anything to do the same to Magus, but she was nothing more than a night bug under his heel.

A small pebble tick-tick-ticked as it skidded along the stone road, rolling to a rest next to her foot. She whirled to her left, hand outstretched and the fire of mezhik at her fingertips. Her dark-purple cloak twisted and fluttered behind her.

Large, glowing eyes shone from the shadows a dozen paces away.

CHAPTER TWO

Emorith's ailing heart drummed in her ears, a cacophony against the deathly quiet night. The hairs on her nape stood erect as she searched the darkness for the pebble's source. Orange flames rose from her palm, lapping at the air as they formed into a fireball.

Her hand slid several inches down the shaft of her staff, a better position in case she needed to use it as a club. She hoped she'd need neither the staff nor the fireball. She took several moments and a deep breath to reign in her fear as best she could and to steel her resolve before addressing the darkness.

"Step out of the shadows, or I'll end your life." Her voice still quavered. She chided herself but kept her focus on the shadows.

Farther to her left than she'd thought, she sensed movement. She turned quickly, separating herself from the potential threat with the fireball. A small-statured man stepped into the flickering light, his glowing, green eyes wide, and his gaze locked onto the fireball.

The man wore a white, tattered shirt that hung low on his narrow, sloped shoulders and matched his pasty, white skin. His long, slender arms were little more than twigs protruding from the short sleeves, and his lanky fingers nearly touched his bare, bony knees.

He pressed closer and reached toward the flames. "Eshtak touch?"

Emorith gasped. "Wizard's fire?" She closed her hand, extinguishing the flame. "Are you mad?"

The man looked up at her and frowned, his chin non-existent. "Eshtak happy, not mad." He grinned wide, stretching his thin, black lips ear-to-ear and baring a mouthful of yellowed teeth.

"I suppose—" He grabbed her hand, and she swallowed down a yelp. "Hey!"

He paid her no attention as he pried her fingers up, one by one. With her last finger straightened, he stared at her palm and then turned her hand over. "Light gone?" He looked up at her. "Pretty lady show?"

She laughed. How long had it been since anyone had called her pretty other than Illian? Far longer than she'd have liked. She bent down and perched on her tippy toes, matching the little man's eye level.

"I'm Emorith. Your name's Eshtak?"

He beat his chest proudly with the palm of his hand. "Eshtak." He spun in a circle.

Eshtak reminded her so much of Illian when he was younger, but she guessed Eshtak to be far older than he acted.

Are all the dwellers so simple-minded?

They must be.

It's probably why Magus chose Intus.

Magus loathed children. To be truthful, he loathed all creatures lacking mezhik, deeming them little more than fodder for war. Lesser races, like the dwellers, would be eradicated if Magus controlled the entire Ancient Realm. Scourge marked the first step in "cleansing the world" as Magus called it. It sickened her, but Illian's life mattered more than anything to her.

She opened her hand. *"Əllíṭ ʊb."* An orange ball of light formed above her palm and lit up a five-foot area around them.

"Ooh!" Eshtak bounced from foot to foot. He stuck his hand out, but only a little. His head tilted. "Eshtak touch?"

She nodded. "This one you can. It's only light, not fire."

Eshtak poked the ball with one finger and recoiled as it floated backward. Emorith moved her fingers and the ball danced in the air. Eshtak watched, enraptured. His eyes bulged and his feet moved with the light. He hummed a tune she'd never heard, its melody far more beautiful than anything she would've thought possible from such a strange, little man.

"What is that song?" she asked.

"Eshtak sings to Mother. Light in big sky." He spread his arms wide.

Emorith looked up. "The crystal?"

"No." The gruff voice came from behind her.

She spun about, her staff raised defensively. Her heart pounded so hard that the arteries in her neck jerked. Mezhik burned in her fingers once again. The stocky man stood a few paces away, a knife blade glinting in the bluish light. She glared at him. "Do you seek death?"

He pointed the knife at her. "Could ask the same of you, sorceress. Your kind ain't welcome here."

Eshtak spun around her, stopping between her and the other man. He held his arms up. "Lady Eshtak's friend. Brother not hurt her."

Brother?

The two of them were polar opposites. The man stood a head length taller than Eshtak and nearly a foot wider, and his muscles bulged where Eshtak's failed to form. Like Eshtak, he had little hair to speak of, but a sinewy scar lined each side of his head from temple to crown. She knew little of the dweller culture, but those marks she recognized.

He's heir to the throne.

Emorith stepped back, lowered her staff, and dipped her head. "Forgive my ignorance, your highness. I am but passing through." She reigned her mezhik back in.

He snarled, "Late hour to be 'passing through,' don't you think?"

Eshtak pushed the man's arm down. "Friend."

The man shoved Eshtak aside and stepped closer, the knife twirling in his hand. "State your business, or this blade will be the last thing you see or feel."

Emorith retreated another step. Had she misjudged these people? Were they not so simple-minded and docile? She took a breath and called her mezhik to her tongue; it burned and soothed at once. "I've not come to hurt you. You don't *need* the knife."

The man's countenance changed abruptly. He cocked his head and then looked down at the knife he held. He frowned at it for several moments as though it were foreign to him and his hand. "Strange…"

He blinked several times, flipped the knife in the air, caught it by its handle, and sheathed it in the sheath that hung from his belt. "Now, where was I?"

Emorith stared into his eyes, two yellowish-green portals that led straight into his mind. She spoke with persuasion. "I've answered all your questions to your satisfaction, and you were about to grant Eshtak permission to show me all the secrets your city holds." She looked at Eshtak and winked. "Wasn't he, Eshtak?"

Eshtak nodded vigorously. "Eshtak loves secrets!"

The man scratched his head and sighed. "Might've been."

She smiled within. *This will be easier than I thought.*

He shook his head. "Truthfully, I'm feeling a tad off tonight. Head's in a bit of a spin."

She leaned heavily on her staff. "You mentioned that, and it certainly seems to be the case. I've yet to hear your name."

"Manners have bested me tonight." He offered her his hand. "Tuvak, son of Aervik The Quiet, our king."

She looked at his large hand. Odd it'd be so rough with him being royalty.

"Emorith Darkridge." She took his hand, and he pulled hers toward his lips. They were thin and black like Eshtak's, but bits of excess skin hung from them and scratched her skin when he pressed them against the top of her hand.

His wet, sticky tongue slithered across her knuckles. She stifled the urge to pull her hand back but cringed within.

Gross!

Bile rose in her throat as his lustful gaze met hers. She swallowed it down and forced a smile as she gently pulled her hand away. "A pleasure."

"Likewise." He moved closer. Too close.

Twice in the past, she'd used her persuasive mezhik too heavily, and the second of those occasions almost cost her life. She quickly learned two lessons that day: a butcher's wife knows her way around her husband's knives, and she doesn't take kindly to the woman attracting her husband's attention. Emorith smirked now, but it had been anything but amusing at the time.

This marked the third time. Tuvak would be enamored with her for hours. She scowled at him. "You don't like being so close to me."

"Don't I?" He backed away a step and pulled at his shirt. "Is it hot in here? It is hot, right?" Beads of sweat pooled on top of his bald, cone-shaped head and formed rivulets as they dripped down the sides of his face.

"Eshtak not hot." He spun in circles. "Eshtak show secrets?"

"No," growled Tuvak. "Secrets are mine to show."

Eshtak stopped spinning and hung his head. "Eshtak's friend first." He shrank back toward the shadows where he'd come from.

Emorith needed to regain control of the situation before everything fell apart. Eshtak would be the more malleable test subject and less likely to be missed. "Eshtak, come back."

Eshtak stopped and looked back at her. Tears filled his eyes.

She turned and smiled at Tuvak. "Tuvak, you're too tired to show me the secrets. You should go home and get some sleep. By the morning, you'll feel better and remember none of this."

Tuvak yawned and rubbed his eyes, but he was still too enamored with her to leave her presence. "Need sleep but can't leave you alone with Eshtak. We'll all go together."

Eshtak wiped his eyes and smiled. "Eshtak show secrets." He rushed to Emorith's side and grabbed her hand.

Tuvak growled deep, his knife back in his hand. He snarled at Eshtak, "Touch her again, and this blade will find a new home at the center of your heart."

Eshtak let go and shrank away. "Brother not hurt brother!"

"Enough." She pointed a finger at Tuvak. "Put the knife away before you hurt yourself with it." She didn't need to persuade him further.

He complied and grumbled incoherently. He shook a fist at Eshtak. "Show her the best fishing spots and the best place to purchase wares and food, but none of your hidden passage nonsense. I ain't got all night."

Emorith's eyebrows rose and so did her voice. "Hidden passages? Sounds far more intriguing than fishing holes and shops." She eyed Eshtak. "Where do these passages lead?"

"Away!" Eshtak spun in a circle with his arms spread wide.

She turned to Tuvak. "There's another way to leave Intus besides the main road?"

"No," grumbled Tuvak.

Eshtak stopped spinning, nodded, and bounced around. "Yes, yes, yes! Eshtak show."

"He's a bumbling fool and don't know what he's talking about." Tuvak shook his head. "There's a reason our city lies beneath the mountain. We are a peaceful race, but we're far from ignorant. We can seal off the entrance into Intus and defend it if needed, but we have other means of protection as well." He crossed his arms over his chest. "Don't *need* another way out."

"Come, come, come!" Eshtak raced forward and into the shadows.

She ignored Eshtak's further prompts to follow and instead turned her attention back to Tuvak. "What other means?"

His eyes glanced upward for the briefest moment, but he said nothing. Emorith's pulse quickened.

The aethershard crystal.

"How does the crystal protect you?"

Tuvak rubbed the back of his neck, his eyes betraying him yet again. "Never said it was the crystal."

She pushed harder, without using her persuasion. "You're not a good liar. Your eyes keep looking up at it. Tell me, what does it do?"

He stared at the ground. "Father would banish me if I told you anything else."

She moved close and lifted his head until his gaze finally met hers. "He doesn't need to know. The secret will stay between us. I promise."

"Eshtak not tell. Eshtak loves secrets."

She looked over her shoulder at Eshtak. "Okay, it'll stay between the three of us." She turned and met Tuvak's gaze again. "Tell me about the crystal."

Tuvak sighed. "Very well, but explaining everything might take some time."

Emorith leaned on her staff. "I don't need to know the entire history of the crystal. Just the highlights will suffice."

"Our high priest controls the crystal with mezhik."

She'd never heard of the dwellers having their own religion, let alone a high priest. More to the point, she'd thought they were all onzhifţäd. This knowledge could change everything.

But how can I use it to my advantage?

"How is this possible?"

Tuvak shrugged. "Same way as you, I suppose."

She shook her head. "That's not what I mean. Do others of your kind wield mezhik as well?"

"Not dweller," said Eshtak. "Outside man."

The revelation stunned her. How had an outsider become their high priest when they kept to themselves so fiercely? Especially a wizard?

Does Magus know?

"You don't know that," scolded Tuvak.

Eshtak frowned and crossed his arms. "Eshtak knows. Eshtak hears man."

Tuvak took a swipe at Eshtak's head, but Eshtak proved far quicker and easily avoided his assault. "Get back here, you little liar."

Eshtak's face scrunched up. "Eshtak not liar. Brother liar."

Emorith spread her arms wide. "Ugh! Enough bickering."

The two of them froze, both wide-eyed. Neither said another word. *Good.*

A strong breeze swept across the road, kicking up a chill that drove into her bones. She drew the sides of her cloak tight. "Can I meet this priest?"

"No," said Tuvak.

She fought the urge to persuade him once more, but she needed to know everything about the crystal. Somehow, it held the answers she sought. Her gut told her as much. The key to hers and Illian's future hung two thousand feet above her head.

"You must—"

Tuvak held up his hand and cut her off. "No one has access to the high priest other than the king. Not even me." He rubbed his chin. "Everything we know of him is based purely on speculation."

Emorith circled her staff. "Are you saying that you don't know how he controls the crystal?"

"As I said before, through mezhik, but I ain't got specific knowledge." Tuvak paced. "If Intus is invaded, he can erect a mezhik barrier using the crystal. That barrier will surround the entire city like a bubble and cannot be breached—from either side. Anyone will be incinerated if they cross through it."

"Using teleportation as well?"

Tuvak shrugged. "Suppose."

A plan started taking shape in Emorith's mind but to what end she wasn't sure. *Yet.*

She turned to Eshtak. "Show me this other way to leave Intus."

Tuvak huffed, "Doesn't exist."

She glanced back at Tuvak. "Feel free to find your way home."

Eshtak took Emorith's outstretched hand and pulled her along the granite slab road, farther into the depths of Intus. Tuvak followed close behind, grumbling disapproval with every step.

† † †

Forty minutes later, Emorith, Eshtak, and Tuvak stood in front of a thirty-foot-tall building. Its architecture differed from the other buildings spread across the city, and its pure-white stone façade stood in stark contrast to the dark stones used everywhere else.

Three wide steps led up to a portico, and ten marble pillars rose to meet the triangular pediment above. Ancient runes, chiseled from green, red, and yellow precious stones, adorned the face of the otherwise plain pediment. The temple backed up to a sheer wall of stone a hundred feet high.

Tuvak glared at Eshtak. "You led us to the Temple of *Eallizenōz*? Why? I know this building front-to-back. No secrets are hidden within its walls."

Eallizenōz...

Emorith had studied the gods of old when she lived amongst Fekɛzhn dhä Räd, a religious sect that took in orphans and worshiped Ɂäṭūr as the only God. However, they'd never mentioned one named Eəllizenōz. Based on everything around her, she guessed it to be some sort of stone god.

But why the white stone?

Eshtak huffed, "Eshtak show." He jerked Emorith's arm so hard that she nearly fell over as she stumbled sideways.

She pulled back until he stopped. "Careful, little guy. My arm's not meant to detach from my body."

Eshtak released her hand. His lower lip trembled. "Eshtak sorry. Not mean to hurt friend."

She rubbed the top of his smooth head. "It's okay. I know you didn't. Just be gentler in the future."

He nodded. "Friend follow Eshtak." He raced over to the left side of the temple and disappeared around the corner.

Tuvak grabbed a handful of Emorith's cloak as she turned to follow Eshtak. "You're wasting your time."

She turned back. "Am I?"

He gazed up at her. "Perhaps it'd be better spent *alone* in my company. I could give you a personal tour of my bedchambers." He winked at her. "If you understand my meaning."

Don't blame him, Emorith. It's only the persuasion talking.

But when would it run its course?

She smiled. "Oh, I'm certain I understand your meaning. And, as intrigued as I may be of your generous offer, I must decline." She jerked her cloak from his grasp. "Perhaps another time when I'm not in such a hurry."

She turned and walked toward the corner of the building.

"Your loss," said Tuvak.

I'm certain it's not.

She reached the corner and peered into the deep shadows around it. Nothing moved. She looked back. Tuvak still stood in front of the temple, his arms crossed tight over his chest and a scowl on his face.

"Are you not coming?"

Tuvak shook his head. "No point. Ain't nothing back there but rock."

She shrugged. "Suit yourself."

Emorith took a few steps into the shadows before the darkness swallowed her. She stopped, but her head wobbled on her neck and churned the contents of her stomach. She couldn't see her own hand in front of her face. How Eshtak moved through perfect darkness baffled her. She needed assistance.

"*Əllị̇t ʊb.*" An orange ball of light formed in her palm, tearing the veil of darkness before her. "That's better."

The ball soared overhead and moved a few feet out in front of her. It kept pace with her as she made her way through the narrow gap between the temple and the building next to it. Several hundred feet in, she finally spotted the temple's back corner just ahead.

Eshtak's green eyes glowed in the darkness as the light met them. He awaited her arrival at the corner, his eyes bobbing up and down as he hopped from one foot to the other. When she arrived, he slipped into the darkness around the corner.

The light preceded her as she rounded the back corner of the temple, but the only thing she found back there was a wall of rock ten paces ahead. She proceeded to the rock wall, but no path or doorway existed. Neither did Eshtak.

She turned back, thinking she'd missed something, but the temple wall and the rock wall running parallel to it both looked solid. "Eshtak?"

"Eshtak here."

Her heart jumped into her throat as she spun back around. Eshtak stood in front of the rock wall at the end of the narrow passage.

"This way. Come!" He stepped to the side—away from the temple—and disappeared into the rock wall.

Mezhik?

She moved toward the corner, her light leading the way, and that's when she finally saw it. Only about ten inches wide, the narrow gap blended right in with the surrounding walls. She had to be right on it to see it, and even then, it seemed to disappear when she stared at it for more than a moment.

She squeezed through the gap, and then traversed a steep incline up into a rectangular chamber about five feet wide and twelve feet deep. The ceiling hung a little more than a foot above her head, lined with jagged rock. Iron sconces hung from the walls on both sides of the chamber.

She closed her palm and snuffed out her ball of orange light, and then she called upon her mezhik once more. *"Ɛäţ äbəlläíz."*

Fire shot from her fingertips and ignited the six torches placed inside the sconces. Burning pitch filled her nostrils, but only for a moment. A draught from somewhere she couldn't identify drew the smoke from the chamber.

Eshtak clapped and pirouetted and danced in circles. Emorith shook her head.

Such a strange, little man.

"This is interesting, but where's the…" Her voice trailed off as her gaze fell upon the mirror mounted in the wall at the back of the chamber.

She strode forward, gently pushing past Eshtak, and stopped in front of the mirror. Had it not reflected her image, she would've missed it altogether. No frame surrounded it. In fact, the mirror's jagged edges blended right into the surrounding rock.

Intus held more secrets than she'd thought possible when she arrived a few hours earlier. So many thoughts filled her mind on how she might use her newfound knowledge to her advantage, but none would free her and Illian from Magus.

She moved closer to the mirror. "You know what this mirror does?"

Eshtak nodded. "Wizard portal."

Ages ago, wizards used ancient mezhik techniques lost to the present world to create several mirrors, or portals, across the Ancient Realm to make traveling great distances easier. Perhaps the mirrors existed in other realms as well, but she didn't know. No one knew how many of them truly existed.

A single thought of destination and the touch of its surface would open the portal. However, only the zhifţäd, those who possessed mezhik, could use them. If an unzhifţäd used a mirror they would turn to ash on the other side.

Emorith took note of the small wrinkles extending from the corners of her eyes and the edges of her lips. She squeezed her pale cheeks, bringing color back into them, but the effect faded quickly.

Just like the years have.

She couldn't recall at what point she'd become a woman, but little remained of the young girl she remembered herself to be. A single strand of silver hair curled down her left cheek, contrasting her head of raven locks. She reached up to yank it out but thought better of it. It would change nothing.

Little blue and orange flames flickered in her dark eyes. Perhaps nothing more than reflections of torchlight, but she couldn't dismiss the notion that they resembled her tortured soul.

Eshtak stood next to her, a fistful of her cloak clutched in his hand. It reminded her of Illian and tightened her throat. His gaze met hers through the mirror's reflection.

Tears glistened on Eshtak's cheeks. "Friend leave?"

Each moment bonded her with Eshtak further, weakening her resolve on what she knew must be done. Guilt twisted her stomach, but she must put Illian first. No one and nothing else mattered.

She offered him a sad smile. "Not just yet, but soon."

He nodded and lowered his head. "Eshtak will miss."

Her heart ached. She closed her eyes for a few moments and focused her mind on the task at hand.

I will keep you safe, Illian.

She swallowed down her growing feelings for Eshtak and locked her heart inside a steel cage within her mind.

I am above feeling anything.

She repeated it in her mind several times, but the lie would not take hold. Even though she knew lying to herself wouldn't work, she still sighed.

She refocused on the mirror.

Does it still work?

One way to find out...

Emorith thought of home—or at least the only place she identified as home—and reached toward the mirror but stopped short of touching its surface as several questions crept into her mind.

Who else knows about this mirror? Who used it last? Did they come here or leave from here? Where will it lead if I don't influence the destination and just touch it?

She might never know the answer to most of her questions, but she could at least find out where it last led. She focused on her own reflection and cleared her mind of all thoughts. Satisfied, she reached out and touched the mirror's surface with the palm of her hand. The surface rippled, became cold and wet underneath her palm, and then the reflected room faded into darkness.

The darkness in the mirror swirled as light and color began replacing it. A long hallway with thick, brown carpets and drab green walls materialized through the mirror and stretched into the distance. Eshtak gasped and latched onto her leg.

Several pairs of double doors with white trim lined either side of the hallway, and ornate sconces flanked each of them. Candles burned in just a few of them, leaving parts of the hallway unlit. A man dressed in brown trousers and a white, billowed shirt stepped into the hallway, his back to them. A wide mohawk of straw-yellow hair striped his dark-skinned head.

"Auh!" Emorith pulled her hand away from the mirror and covered her mouth.

The man jerked upright, froze for a moment, and then turned toward them. His gaze, focused on the floor, traversed the length of the hallway as his head rose.

Emorith stuttered backward, her gaze locked onto the clean-shaven face of a man she thought long dead. His eyes met hers, and then the world beyond the mirror faded to black.

She dropped to her knees and pulled against the part of her cloak that swaddled her neck, suddenly fighting for air. The chamber sweltered and her skin beaded with sweat. A fine mist filmed her eyes, built into pools, and spilled down her cheeks.

The mirror returned the chamber's reflection once more, but her mind clung to the image of the man's grey eyes.

Ansgar?

No, it isn't possible.

He'd died. She'd witnessed it. A dagger thrust into his belly before he plunged into the dark waters of the Vastus Ocean.

It can't be him.

"Friend knows man?"

So lost within, Emorith had forgotten she wasn't alone. She wiped her face with her sleeves. "I… I don't know. I don't think it can be."

"Man knows friend. Eshtak sees."

The night Ansgar died she'd prayed to the gods to save him. Had one of them answered her prayer? If so, what did it mean? If Ansgar lived, why hadn't he come back for her?

She gazed intently not at but through the mirror, willing it to ripple and meld back into the hallway she'd seen through it, but its surface remained still. Had he not seen her? No, his gaze had met hers. She was certain of it.

Why doesn't he come to me?

Her heart cried out for him, just as it had that night. Her hand shook with uncontrollable violence as she reached toward the mirror, but she couldn't force herself to touch it again. If the man she saw through the mirror proved nothing more than a trick of light, her heart would break all over again.

She didn't trust herself or her eyes, the risk to her heart far too great. She lowered her arm and sat back on the hard ground. Her head pulsed with a dull pain.

But Eshtak saw him too.

She balled her hand.

No, Emorith, it doesn't matter. Illian is all that does. Focus.

She pulled herself to her feet. In another life she would've relished the simplicity in which Eshtak viewed the world, but the fate of the gods didn't favor any of them. She looked at the mirror one last time.

They never have.

Emorith turned away from the mirror and steeled her heart and mind.

Do what must be done.

"Have you ever been outside the cavern?" she asked.

Eshtak shook his head. "Eshtak too afraid. Bad things outside."

She bent down. "Am I bad?"

Eshtak hopped from foot to foot, a similar dance Illian performed when he needed to urinate. "No, no, no! Friend not bad."

"Good. Would you like to see some more mezhik?" Eshtak's head bobbed up and down. "Then come with me to the outside and I'll show you mezhik no one else has ever seen."

"Outside not safe."

"I promise I'll protect you." She reached out and Eshtak took her hand. "Do you trust me?"

He nodded. "Friend not lie."

Gods… Why is this so hard?

She knew the answer.

Because he's like Illian. But he's not my son.

An easy sacrifice would not be a sacrifice at all.

That's all he is.

"You want to take a journey with me and see great feats of mezhik." She'd used her persuasion on him, and it twisted her stomach in knots.

Eshtak peered up at her, his eyes bright and full of wonder. "Eshtak loves journey, especially with friend."

I'm not your friend.

She hated herself for what she did and must do.

A weary smile curved her lips. "Good. There's someone I'd like you to meet."

As Emorith and Eshtak exited the chamber, she pulled the fire from the torches with her mezhik, casting the chamber back into darkness once more. Eshtak guided them through the narrow passage behind and around the side of the temple. When they emerged on the road in front of the temple, they found Tuvak sound asleep on the temple steps.

Across the city, at the top of the switchback road that rose to meet the tunnel in the side of the mountain, a faint yet noticeable light filtered in.

Dawn.

She turned to Eshtak. "We must make haste."

He pointed at Tuvak. "Brother comes?"

"Not this time, but we'll be back soon." Emorith let go of his hand.

Eshtak nodded. "Eshtak knows shortcut. Saves time."

"Fine." She swept her arm toward the road. "Lead the way out of here. I'll be right behind you."

He bounded down the road, arms stretched wide, and headed toward damnation with a smile on his face. Guilt gurgled in the pit of her stomach, but the fateful future of Intus could not be avoided. At least not without sacrificing Illian, and that would never be an option.

CHAPTER THREE

Dawn passed into morning and then into the early afternoon as Emorith and Eshtak arrived at the edge of camp. She led him through a sea of tents, toward the largest one located in the center of the camp—Magus's tent.

In a camp of five hundred, Emorith was one of only four women. Two of the women were sorceresses like her, and the other a governess named Javana. Javana watched over Illian while Emorith performed tasks for Magus. Illian was the only child among them, a pawn with which Magus controlled Emorith.

Soldiers moved about throughout the camp, some sharpening weapons and others gathering wood for the night. A few stood around fires, preparing the afternoon meal. The rest of them watched the perimeter and scouted the area for enemy combatants.

A campaign such as this, carried out on enemy soil, defied logic—at least in her mind. They certainly had the personnel and skills to defend themselves in a skirmish, but the risk of their five hundred standing against an entire kingdom bent on eradicating mezhik would prove fatal. Such an event would change the landscape of the Ancient Realm forever.

Black flags donning two white fangs with blood dripping from them hung outside Magus's tent, flanking its wide opening. Soldiers stood to either side of the opening as well, stoic statues dressed in black, shining armor. Each held a pike in their left hand, and a sword hung from their left hip. The flags stirred in the late morning breeze, rustling and snapping with each strong gust.

Emorith and Eshtak stepped inside the tent and halted. She released his hand and wiped hers on her trousers. Eshtak peered up at her, and she held a finger to her lips. He nodded, his eyes wide and his sunken chin trembling.

Magus stood a good twenty paces ahead, leaning over a large, wooden table with his back to them. Tight, black leathers hugged his muscular form, quite a departure from his usual grey robes, yet they suited him. From her angle, she could just make out his set jaw, lined with grey stubble.

Angry, as usual.

Emorith looked to the floor. If required, she'd wait there until dusk just to keep from interrupting him. She knew better. His temper flared easily and giving him another excuse to harm Illian was the last thing she needed or wanted.

Magus's baritone voice drove into her chest. "You were gone far longer than necessary."

He baited her. She would wait.

Magus straightened and faced her. His gaze fell on Eshtak for a few brief moments and then returned to meet hers. "I take it you had success."

A statement, not a question.

She continued to wait. Ten years with Magus taught her great discipline.

Magus halved the distance in three strides. "Did persuading it prove difficult?"

She stood there a mute, her throat constricted.

Open your mouth and answer him!

She struggled but found her voice. "On the contrary, my liege." The false title soiled her tongue, leaving behind the foul taste of excrement. "The task proved hardly an effort."

Magus brooded. "Does it understand its role in our plan?"

None of this is part of my *plan.*

She'd give almost anything to speak her mind but wouldn't dare for fear of what Magus would do to Illian.

"No, my liege, but he is of simple mind. He won't present a problem for us. I'll make certain of it when the time comes."

Magus's nose wrinkled, and he swatted at the air. "Ugh. Remove that thing from my tent before its stench becomes a permanent fixture on the linens." He turned and walked back over to the table. "And make sure it gets bathed. Everything must be ready by dusk."

Emorith dipped her head. "My liege." She took Eshtak's hand and escorted him out of the tent.

Outside, Eshtak pulled his hand away and squirmed and shook violently. "Bad, bad man. Eshtak not like. Eshtak scared." He pulled down on his cheeks, making his large eyes bulge further.

As am I.

Emorith forced a smile and rubbed his head. "It's okay. No harm will come to you as long as you do as I ask. Do you understand?"

He nodded. "Eshtak trusts friend."

Every time Eshtak used the word "friend," it socked her in the stomach. She'd give almost anything to send him back home, but the gods had plans for them all. She needed to stay focused.

Remember the goal. Save Illian, no matter the cost.

She took his hand. "Come on. I think it's time you met my son, Illian. I'm sure he's due for a bath as well."

Eshtak sniffed his armpits and stuck out his lower lip. "Eshtak not need bath."

She squeezed his hand. "Don't think of it as a bath. It's an adventure."

Eshtak skipped along next to her. "Eshtak loves adventure."

"I know you do. Now, let's go find Illian and head to the springs."

✝ ✝ ✝

In all of thirty seconds, Eshtak and Illian had become fast friends. Emorith sat back and watched them from the edge of the springs as she soaked her feet in its soothing waters. She longed for a day where she could enjoy life the way they did, wrestling and splashing through the water without a care in the world, but she knew it would never come.

Not while I remain under Magus's heel.

The more time she spent with Eshtak the weaker her resolve grew and the deeper her agony became. How could Magus be willing to destroy so many innocent lives? The dwellers lived away from the world and oppressed no one.

When she'd met Magus, he'd talked of a world full of peace and harmony, but neither of those things existed in his new vision for Centauria. Now, every conversation revolved around bringing down the vile and traitorous ʊnzhiftäd, King Ordin, who ruled the northern half of the Ancient Realm.

Both men drank power and bred hatred in their own right. In her mind, neither served the people nor their kingdoms. In the end, greed would destroy them both, or so she hoped.

She lay back in the thick, silvered grass and closed her eyes. How had her life taken such a treacherous path? She'd been happy once, hadn't she? Those grey eyes in the mirror behind the temple haunted her. Her life ended the day Ansgar perished, and she never thought she'd be happy again, but then Illian came into her life and restarted her cold, dead heart.

Intus threatened her happiness once again. She would not relinquish it without a fight.

They must die so that he can live.

She opened her eyes. The late afternoon sun hung below the tree line to the east, and darkness crept upon the landscape. She must've drifted off to sleep.

She pulled her feet from the water. Never had she seen them so wrinkled. She shook the water from them and rolled her stocking on. With a few grunts, she managed to pull her calf-high boots on and then laced them up.

She grabbed her staff and pulled herself to her feet. She scanned the springs and the small pond but didn't see Eshtak or Illian. Her breath caught.

Did Magus take them?

Emorith turned around and found them lying in the grass a few feet beyond her, arm-in-arm and fast asleep. She breathed easier. Tonight, Illian's heart would break for Eshtak, but at least he'd be safe again.

For how long though?

She knew the answer. Magus would eventually kill her and Illian.

I must find a way out.

She woke Eshtak and Illian, and the three of them returned to the camp.

While they were gone, the soldiers had cleared away a large circle, perhaps thirty feet in diameter, in front of Magus's tent, all the way down to the beige, rocky soil. Not a single sprig of grass remained. In place of the grass rose several mounds of black sand shipped straight from Incendia Island.

Known to be the purest sand in the world, its black color came from deep within the planet's core and straight up through the Vulcan Caldera. Legend claimed it to be the remnants of dragon's fire.

Often, rune mezhik stemmed from mezhik derk, a type of mezhik practiced by wizards and sorceresses bent on destruction. The world banned mezhik derk decades ago, yet many still practiced it. On rare occasions, such as this one, both sides of mezhik would be used to try to achieve what Magus called a spell of legend: bräkärᴣbäəll.

Eshtak would be the test subject for the immunity spell and Intus the testbed for scourge, a spell so devastating that it would rip souls from the living and thrust their bodies into a place Magus deemed "the between," where they would roam aimlessly until the Great Separation.

Bräkärᴣbäəll, if achieved, would provide anyone or anything protection from all types of mezhik, effectively rendering mezhik useless against them. To be able to wield mezhik and yet be protected from it would turn a person into a god. Magus sought to be just that.

If the campaign proved successful, Magus would use bräkärᴣbäəll to protect himself and other wizards and sorceresses from scourge when they unleashed it on the Ancient Realm. However, if the campaign failed, there would be hell to pay for everyone involved.

Gorath and Morlar, two of Magus's most trusted wizards, began spreading the sand evenly across the circle, creating a base on which the rune spell would be drawn.

Rune mezhik required special elements, crushed into a fine dust, to achieve spells beyond any that could be merely spoken. The dust would be used to draw intricate patterns known as runes on top of the base. Each rune must be precise for its effect to be achieved. One errant line could alter the desired spell and potentially kill all those involved.

Gorath and Morlar finished spreading the sand evenly and stepped out of the black sand circle. A dozen soldiers with torch poles moved forward and surrounded the circle's perimeter, their torches lit and the smell of burning pitch ripe in the air.

Emorith begged the gods to make the immunity spell fail to protect Eshtak, not because she wished him dead but because she feared for the rest of the world, including herself and Illian. If Eshtak survived, the world would be damned and everything she'd done in the name of protecting Illian would have been for nothing. She couldn't live with that.

She stood back several feet from the circle, Illian latched onto her left side and Eshtak her right. Magus stepped into the circle and moved to its center. Everyone in the camp fell silent.

Magus's eyes gleamed in the firelight, a demon hellbent on destruction. He motioned Eshtak forward.

Emorith looked down and met Eshtak's gaze. Fear filled his eyes. She handed Illian her staff and bent down. "It's okay, Eshtak. You have nothing to fear. When this is finished, we'll take you back home."

Eshtak looked at the circle and then toward Intus. "Eshtak not stay. Eshtak goes home now."

Emorith grabbed his shoulders and peered into his green eyes. The power of persuasion burned on her tongue, and the thought of using it on Eshtak again sickened her, but she had no other choice.

She drew upon her mezhik and spoke to his heart. "You want to do this, Eshtak. It will be fun. You love mezhik."

His chin quivered, and he shook his head. "Eshtak not want."

His resistance surprised her.

Perhaps Tuvak would've made the better choice.

It didn't matter now. She changed her tactic and pushed harder, knowing the consequence of failure. "Doing this will help save Tuvak." The lie twisted her stomach and blackened her heart further. "Is that not what you want?"

"Save brother?"

"He won't live if you don't do this."

Eshtak looked over at Magus. "Eshtak scared."

"I know, but I'll be right here with Illian. We won't leave you."

Tears wet his cheeks. He nodded. "Eshtak do for brother. Eshtak do for friend."

Backstabber, not a friend.

Emorith bit down hard on the inside of her cheek to hold back her tears. Blood filled her mouth. She swallowed it down and bit harder still. She nudged Eshtak toward the circle. He looked back for a moment and then stepped into the circle.

Magus positioned Eshtak in the center of the circle, and then he addressed the crowd of wizards and sorceresses. "Tonight, my brothers and sisters, we take another step toward the future."

They all cheered, including Emorith, but her heart feared the future more than anything. She pulled Illian close and held his head against her side. *For you, my son.*

Magus continued, "However, there are a few more steps to follow before we truly have reason to cheer. So let us hold fast to this path we're on and may we find favor with the gods in the goals we've set forth to achieve."

"To the gods!" they cried.

Magus bent down and said something to Eshtak, but Emorith didn't hear what he'd said. Magus stood and pulled a large leather bag from within the folds of his robes. He opened the top of the bag, reached into it, and pulled out a handful of white sand. With it, he drew a perfect circle around Eshtak.

Magus proceeded to draw ten straight lines outward from the white circle, like spokes of a wagon wheel, each spaced an equal distance apart. The lines stopped four feet from the outer edge of the black sand circle. With that complete, he drew another circle just inside the outer perimeter of the black sand circle and stubbed in one-foot lines inside of it that would've connected to their corresponding lines were he to have continued them. In all, exactly three feet separated each of the lines from joining together.

Magus inspected his work, nodded to himself, and then he turned his attention back to the crowd. He raised his arms. "Brothers, sisters, those called upon for this task, step forward and take your place."

One by one, nine wizards stepped into the black sand circle and positioned themselves between each set of broken white lines. The spell required ten distinct types of mezhik, hers being one of them. In so many ways, she was the key to everything. Imōzzhn, the type of mezhik she possessed, was rare, so much so that no two wizards or sorceresses in history existed simultaneously with it.

Refusing to participate would stop the campaign from moving forward, but the cost would devastate her. Magus would make her watch as he tortured and killed Illian, and then he would use her until it killed her. The only choice she had was to participate.

She kissed Illian's head, released him into Javana's care, and stepped into the circle. She took her position between the last of the broken lines and breathed deep. Her gaze met Eshtak's. He stood perfectly still, his cheeks wet with tears as he smiled warily.

She looked skyward.

Let this fail and let him die. For Illian and Intus.

Magus walked the outer circle's perimeter, handing out daggers and bags filled with the dust of various elements that corresponded with the mezhik type of each wizard or sorceress. Once finished, he stepped back several feet. The rest of those gathered followed his lead.

"Draw your runes!" Magus's voice thundered.

Emorith pulled her bag open and peered inside. An orange dust filled the bag and smelled of fresh clay. She recognized it immediately.

Pherodine.

The single element her kind could control. A dangerous move on Magus's part. Her pulse increased. She could use it to tear him asunder. She looked back at Illian. Magus stood next to Illian, his hand resting on Illian's shoulder.

Her heart sank.

Do what must be done.

She knelt and began drawing her heart-shaped rune with the pherodine. Even strokes. Perfect lines and curves. The butt of the heart—its top—joined with the white line attached to the innermost white circle, and the pointed end of the heart joined with the stubbed end of the white line attached to the outermost white circle, forming a continuous pathway for the mezhik to travel.

Once finished, Emorith watched the other nine wizards as they did the same in succession, each drawing a rune that matched their mezhik type.

Qordis, a bald, young, light wizard with skin dark as night, drew a yellow sun representing Fizärd Əllíṭ. After him came Verdan, a nature wizard. The old man drew the green leaf of Fizärd Näíṭəzhär. The grey claw of Fizärd Enämäəll surrounded Amsel, an animal wizard. Emorith wondered what it would be like to speak with animals and spirit walk with them.

A brown mountain formed around Morlar, an earth wizard, representing Fizärd Ōírdh. The brown substance matched his earthy, brown robes and skin. Trizen, an air wizard, drew the white wind gust of Fizärd Erzíe around himself. His long, windswept hair billowed behind him like a white flag.

Gorath, a self-proclaimed master of fire, growled as he drew a dark-red flame in the sand. A Fizärd Fír, he scared Emorith almost as much as Magus. After him came Urdan, Gorath's polar opposite. Urdan could do things with water that Emorith thought impossible. He drew a blue water droplet around himself, representing Fizärd Fūṭär.

Shira, an illusionist and the only other sorceress in the group of ten, drew a reddish-white optical triangle with the elements from her bag. Her bright-red robes matched her short-cropped hair. A Fizärd Iəllūəzhän, you could never trust your eyes around her.

Kordel, a prophet wizard, drew his rune last. Representing Fizärd Brefäṭ, his rune took the shape of a purplish eye. He doubled as a scribe, recording the events without bias.

Magus walked around the outer black sand circle and inspected each rune. Satisfied, he took the bag from each wizard and sorceress and tossed them aside.

"Center yourselves inside your runes," Magus commanded. Each of them complied. "Good. Now take the dagger and pierce your flesh."

Emorith eyed the dagger and then her open palm. Sweat glistened on her palm. She closed her eyes.

For Illian.

She opened her eyes and drew the dagger across her palm. She felt only a pinch, the blade razor-sharp. Blood pooled over the wound. She cupped her hand to keep it from dripping.

Magus paced around the black sand circle. "Add your blood to your runes and call upon the name of your mezhik."

Emorith turned in a circle, letting the blood drip from her hand and onto the orange, heart-shaped rune. Ten drops fell in total, each sizzling on contact. She faced the center of the inner circle once more.

Tears streaked Eshtak's cheeks and wet his tattered shirt. She drew her mezhik from within and persuaded Eshtak to think of it as an adventure. He nodded and complied with a big smile.

May you find peace.

Emorith stretched her arm toward Eshtak. An orange light curled around her fingers. "*Imōzzhn,*" she cried. The others called upon the name of their mezhik as well, a chorus of voices.

Tendrils of mezhik flowed from her hand, stretched across the expanse between her and Eshtak, and slithered around him. The others' mezhik joined hers, cocooning Eshtak in a rainbow of colors so bright that Emorith could no longer see him. The ground quaked and then each rune erupted with a glowing light that shot straight into the air, ten beacons against the black sky.

The white sand circles and lines pulsated with light, cycling between white and each of the other colors. Like lightning, a wave of light swept inward from the outer circle of white sand to the inner circle of white sand, burning up the runes and lines as it swept past and extinguishing the light and tendrils of mezhik flowing from each wizard and sorceress. As one, the ten of them dropped to their knees, spent of energy.

Emorith's chest heaved and sweat covered her skin, head to toe. It took every ounce of her remaining strength to keep her head upright. The inner circle glowed with such intensity she had to shield her eyes, a task that proved all but impossible in her current state.

A concussive wave ripped the air and expanded outward from the inner circle, bringing a wall of light and black sand with it. It swept over Emorith, knocking her backward and onto her back. It also snuffed out the torchlight, casting the entire camp into darkness, save the inner circle's light. But then its light waned and faded altogether. Eshtak crumpled to the ground and didn't move.

Gods, let him be dead.

Emorith rolled onto her hands and knees and crawled over to Eshtak. Steam rose from his skin, and his chest slowly rose and fell, but he didn't respond to her voice. Intricate patterns of black circles, lines, shapes, and symbols covered Eshtak's stark-white skin, runes as old as the world itself.

A web of mezhik...

Emorith touched Eshtak's face and recoiled. "Ouch!"

"Touching him isn't a wise thing to do right now." Magus stood next to her. "All that energy created an unprecedented level of heat. Had it not been from mezhik, he would've combusted."

She collapsed onto her side. "Then he'll live?"

"Certainly."

Why had the gods not listened to her plea?

Because they aren't my gods.

Magus bent down and lifted her into his arms. "You did well, Emorith. Illian thanks you, as do I."

If she had any fight left in her, she would've summoned the remaining pherodine and driven it into his cold heart. As it stood, another burst of mezhik would certainly kill her. She fought to keep her eyelids open, but even that task proved too great.

In the arms of a beast, she drifted into the darkness of sleep and toward the grey eyes of her past.

Emorith's eyelids fluttered but refused to open, the weight of sleep still upon them. But when the smell of musk—of Magus—filled her nostrils, she jolted upright. Her eyelids stuck to her dry eyes when she opened them, peeling back layers of her eye with them. Pain stung her eyes, flushing them with tears, but it was too little too late. She blinked several times and rubbed them, but the sting remained.

The covers fell away, and the cool air prickled her bare flesh. She reached up and covered her breasts with her arm.

"Ah, the dead rises." Magus's voice came from across the room to her left.

She looked in Magus's direction. He stood in front of a full-length mirror, fully nude. Physically, he was a god-of-a-man, chiseled muscles packed on a frame a handful of inches beyond six feet. Slicked-back, silver hair, tucked behind large, rounded ears, rested on broad shoulders. Bronzed skin covered all but his stark-white buttocks. Several scars crossed his torso and wrapped around his left side. A boar attack, he'd told her. From the looks of it, the boar must've been massive.

Through the mirror's reflection, Emorith's gaze lingered where it shouldn't have, and she chided herself for looking, but she had a fond appreciation for the male form. Had that form been of another man, perhaps one with dark skin and grey eyes, she might've found herself enraptured. However, she knew Magus's heart and his appetite for brutality, and the thought of arousing him struck her with fear.

Panic rose in her chest.

Did he violate me again?

She lay naked in his bed and not her own. Fatigue ached in her muscles, but no pain she could discern accompanied it.

Thank the gods.

She took a deep breath and eased back on the bed. They were alone, so she could speak freely. "How long have I been asleep?"

He walked over to the bed. "Almost two full days."

Two days? Gods… The rune spell must've drained my mezhik to the brink of death.

She forced her gaze to meet his. "That explains why I'm famished, but not why I occupy your bed."

"Death nearly took you. I kept you close to make sure he didn't succeed."

"And what of my clothes?"

He pointed toward the other side of the bed. "Just over there." Emorith glanced over and confirmed their location. "At my command, Javana bathed you and washed your clothes."

She dipped her head. "I am indebted to you, my liege."

"Now there's something we can agree upon." He scratched himself, drawing her attention once again to a place it shouldn't be. "Tomorrow night, when you've regained your strength, you will lie with me."

Bile rose in the back of her throat. Lying with him would be the last thing she'd willingly do. She needed a plan to rid herself of him once and for all. She pulled the covers back, swung her legs over the bed's edge, and stood. Darkness filled her vision and spun her head.

The next thing she knew, Magus held her in his strong arms, his warm, sweaty body pressed firmly against hers. The spinning in her head subsided, and the darkness receded from her vision. She tried pushing him away, but he held fast.

Magus backed her up against the side of the bed. "Perhaps we shouldn't wait until tomorrow night." He pushed his knee between her legs. She didn't have the strength to resist.

Ɂäṭūr, or any god, please save me from him!

"My liege." A soldier stood just inside the tent.

Commander Dirth.

Magus's eyes flashed with violence as he pushed Emorith onto the bed and pulled her legs apart. He growled at Commander Dirth, "Leave us, or you will die where you stand."

"I understand, my liege, but you commanded me to inform you of enemy activity, no matter the hour," said Commander Dirth.

Magus snarled, "Wait outside."

Commander Dirth bowed and exited the tent.

Magus grabbed Emorith's legs and lifted her halfway off the bed as he pulled her toward himself.

No, no, no!

Magus grunted and dropped her legs. "We'll finish this tomorrow night, and there will be no interruptions." He stormed across the room and started putting his clothes back on.

Tears formed in the corners of Emorith's eyes, and she quickly wiped them away before Magus saw them. She'd be severely punished if he caught her crying. Nothing angered and aroused him more than tears.

Magus stormed out of the tent and Emorith breathed easier. She rose from the bed, held onto it as another dizzy spell attacked her, and then walked around it and to the chair that held her clothes.

Fully dressed, she left the tent in search of food. The sun hung low in the east, just above the tree line, right in line with her vision. She held her hand over her eyes as a shield, but her nose could've led her to the food had she been blind. Several spits churned over fire pits throughout the camp, each sporting a different kind of beast. The nearest one skewered a large boar, and its succulent smell drew her over to it.

A young soldier tended the spit and straightened when he noticed her. "I-I-I... um... c-care for a t-t-t-taste, Mistress D-Darkridge?"

Thanks to Magus, every one of the soldiers knew her name. She scarcely knew any of theirs beyond the commanders. She wondered if this young man stuttered naturally or if her presence brought it about. In truth, it made no difference.

Emorith needed the energy and mezhik that bloody meat would provide her. She smiled at the young soldier. "A large chunk will suffice. As rare as you can find it."

His eyes grew wide. "R-rare?"

She nodded. "The bloodier the better. Can you do that for me?"

"Y-yes ma-ma'am."

He unsheathed a large dagger and set to work carving out a chunk of flesh from the boar. He ripped it clean from the bone, dropped it into a wooden bowl, and handed it to her.

Blood pooled in the bottom of the bowl.

Perfect.

The soldier watched her with morbid curiosity. She held the chunk of meat in the bowl with her fingers, lifted the bowl to her lips, and tilted her head back.

The boar's blood mixed with the succulent juices from the fat and poured into her open mouth. She swallowed the salty, coppery liquid down like mead, not letting up until the last drop fell from the bowl. Surprisingly, none ran down her chin. She lowered the bowl and licked her lips.

Strength returned to her fatigued muscles and replenished her energy. Mezhik flowed into her fingertips once more with a single thought and the use of it didn't bring her to her knees as it would have before she drank the bloody juices. She scarfed down the chunk of bloody meat in five bites and tossed the bowl back to the soldier.

He stood there, lower jaw unhinged and eyes wide.

Emorith winked at him. "Just what I needed."

She turned and headed to her own tent, not waiting for a response. As she walked, she formulated a plan that might save Illian and the city of Intus, but it would prove quite risky. For her plan to work, she must trust Javana's loyalty. If she had to use her persuasion mezhik on Javana, then there would be no plan because the power only held for a handful of hours at most. Javana never gave Emorith reason not to trust her, but Illian's life would be in her hands.

What other choice do I have?

She needn't think hard to reach the answer, so she pushed the thought from her mind and willed her plan to succeed.

Inside the tent, Illian and Javana played a game of marbles on the floor. From what she saw, Illian led by a sizable margin. She smiled to herself.

He never loses.

"Have you missed me?"

Illian jumped to his feet, his green eyes almost as wide as the grin on his face. "Mother!"

The brown shirt he wore nearly swallowed his small frame. She kept thinking he'd sprout up any day, but perhaps the gods had stunted his growth to further distance him from ill-wanted comparisons to his father. In truth, Illian looked almost nothing like Magus but resembled her in nearly every way.

Illian ran into her outstretched arms. "Magus said you were unwell. Are you feeling better?"

Illian didn't know Magus had fathered him, and Emorith planned to keep it that way. Besides, Magus would kill Illian before owning up to it.

Thank the gods for small favors.

She kissed Illian's forehead. "Much better, now that I'm with you."

Javana rose from the floor and bowed curtly. A flood of straight, whitish-blonde hair flowed down the sides of her slender face, plummeted over narrow shoulders, and splashed below her small waist in frothy curls. A steep, pointed nose rose to meet narrow-set, yellowish-brown eyes.

Javana's piercing gaze, reminiscent of a hawk's, met Emorith's between strands of hair. "Emorith."

Emorith insisted Javana use her proper name and not some meaningless title when addressing her. She also thought it strengthened the bond between them. If not that, Illian certainly did. No one spent more time with Illian than Javana.

Javana walked over to the tent folds. "I will leave you two for now."

Emorith grabbed Javana's arm. "Not yet. There's something we need to discuss first."

Javana nodded. "As you wish."

The three of them moved farther into the tent and settled down on a large bear pelt. Emorith looked to Illian and then to Javana. Both stared at her with an air of curiosity.

Emorith spoke in a hushed tone, "Tonight, we will set in motion a plan to save Illian and Intus."

Illian bit his lower lip. "Is something wrong with me?"

Emorith reached over and cupped his cheek. "No, my son. Something is wrong with the world."

Javana started to speak, but Emorith cut her off. "No more questions until I've laid out the plan. Understood?" They both nodded, albeit with a hint of reluctance. "Good."

Emorith continued, "Pack a few items and as much food as you can carry but be secretive about it. We will leave during the second watch tonight. We'll travel together until we reach the tunnel entrance to Intus. From there, we will split up. The two of you will continue traveling west until you reach Duos Flumen. From there, you will take a riverboat south to East Hotah. Find a place called the Back Door Inn and wait for my arrival. If all goes as planned, I will meet you there in a month or two. If I've still not arrived within three months, assume the worst.

"Javana, I'm counting on you to take care of Illian for me in my stead. I trust few others to keep him safe. Am I right in thinking you're up for the challenge?"

Javana nodded.

Emorith folded her hands in her lap. "Good. Then it's settled."

"Why can't you come with us?" Illian's eyes teared up.

"It wouldn't be safe for the three of us to travel together." Emorith leaned over and wiped tears from Illian's cheeks. "Besides, I have something else to do first."

Javana fidgeted with her nails. "May I ask what that is?"

"I will return to Intus and seek an audience with King Aervik."

Javana's white eyebrows dipped over the bridge of her nose. "To what end?"

Emorith scooted closer. "Do you know of *Äfäralleɀṭinzh*?"

"Ugh. I may be one of the *ʊnzhifṭäd*, but I'm far from ignorant." Her brown-eyed gaze met Emorith's. "It's the aethershard crystal suspended over Intus."

Javana knew more than Emorith thought she would. "Correct, and do you know its purpose? Or at least one of them?"

Javana shrugged. "I must say I do not."

Emorith took Javana's hand and squeezed it, her excitement building as the plan solidified. "The dwellers control the crystal. If threatened or attacked, they can use its power to erect an impenetrable barrier around the city."

Javana frowned. "I see, but how do you intend to gain an audience with their king?"

Emorith smirked. "Simple. I've befriended his son, Tuvak."

"Befriended or persuaded?"

She shrugged. "Does it matter?"

Javana glanced back at the tent flap and then lowered her voice. "Magus will kill you when he finds out what you've done."

Illian pulled on Emorith's sleeve. "Is that true, Mother?"

Emorith ruffled Illian's hair. "No, because Magus won't know until it's too late." She kissed his forehead. "You and Javana will be long gone, and I'll slip away while Magus fumes over the situation."

"Magus is cunning." Javana sighed. "He'll know it was you, and even if he doesn't figure it out before you run, he'll never stop hunting you."

Emorith stared down at the inside of her left wrist and the heart-shaped mark she'd had since she turned sixteen. "I'm prepared for that. I've always been."

Javana took Illian's hand. "You might be, but is he?"

Emorith knew Magus would kill Illian if they stayed, but she'd never voice her fear in front of him. Running would be a hard life, but they'd be alive and together.

"As you said before, you're not ignorant. You know as well as anyone how this ends if we stay." Emorith glared at Javana, steel in her eyes. "Do you wish to be used your entire life and then be discarded like refuse when you're deemed useless?"

Javana's gaze fell to her lap. "That won't happen."

"Look at me." Javana's gaze rose and met hers. Emorith hated being so forceful, but Javana needed to hear the truth she already knew. "Don't be so foolish. The only reason Magus keeps you around is to use what lies between your legs. You're expendable to him. Never forget that."

Javana nodded. "You're right… about all of it." She wiped a tear from the corner of her eye. "I will do as you've requested."

"Good. Prepare yourself for the journey."

Javana rose from the pelt and exited the tent.

"Mother, why must we leave?"

"There are evil and vile forces at work in this world that you're too young to comprehend. One day, when you're older, I will explain everything to you."

"But I just made a new friend." He grabbed both of Emorith's hands. "Can he come with us?"

"That isn't possible. Eshtak belongs here, and we do not."

Illian covered his face with his hands and bawled. "It's not fair."

"I know, but you must trust me, Illian." She rubbed his back. "Were there another way for us to survive, we'd take it."

Illian leaned over, wrapped his arms around her waist, and laid his head in her lap. "I trust you, Mother. I'm just scared. How will I survive without you?"

"It will only be a few months. I promise. Now, wipe your tears and gather only what is necessary. We will leave in a few hours, while the camp sleeps."

† † †

"Where have you been? We should've left an hour ago."

"Does it matter? I'm here now."

What is she hiding?

Emorith grabbed Javana's arm. "I saw you leaving Magus's tent. What were you doing in there?"

Javana looked down at her arm where Emorith gripped it. "It makes no difference."

Emorith shook her. "It does to me, so tell me the truth. Why were you in there with him?"

"Why do you think?" Javana snapped. "You aroused him earlier, exposing yourself the way you did. And, with everything that's going on, he needed a release, so I spread my legs for him so that you wouldn't have to. You should be thanking me, not grilling me on my whereabouts." She jerked her arm away.

Emorith took a deep breath and reigned in her emotions. "You're right, and I'm sorry. I've just been thinking of everything that could go wrong with the plan and then you show up an hour late after visiting Magus's tent. My vivid imagination bested me. Forgive my insolence."

Javana retrieved a large leather bag from the back corner of the tent. "I'm ready."

† † †

Twenty minutes later, Emorith, Illian, and Javana snaked their way through sprawling tents that speckled the small valley nestled within the southeastern slopes of the Sol Deus Mountains. A dark, new moon and thick, black clouds provided perfect cover, but far more soldiers still lurked about in the late hour than Emorith would've liked.

Twice, they avoided a patrol of soldiers by ducking in the bushes, and Emorith breathed easier when they reached the tree line and the cover of the forest. Her reprieve didn't last long as the treacherous landscape ratcheted up the tension in her chest once again as they began their ascent of the wooded and rocky slope. Scree rendered each step dangerous, slowing their pace to what Emorith deemed a crawl. However, they couldn't afford for one of them to fall and injure themselves or, the gods forbid, die, so Emorith made peace with their slow pace.

An hour later, they summited the ridge separating the camp from the solitary entrance into Intus. The view of the valley below stole her breath, a sea of silver speckled with fires and tents. Had the moon been full and not new, she would've had a perfect view of the Incendia Sea to the south. Instead, the sea lay in an inkwell of darkness.

Perhaps another time.

A half-hour longer and she'd be saying goodbye to Illian, possibly for the last time. The thought misted her eyes, and she hoped it didn't prove true, but she had no other choice.

A little farther along the ridge to the north she spotted a sentry, but not before he spotted her. She needed to take care of the situation before it got out of hand. A single fireball could take him out, but the light and noise might alert others.

Emorith looked back at Illian and Javana. "Start the descent, and do not wait for me at the bottom."

She couldn't handle looking at the terror in Illian's eyes, so she turned and headed toward the sentry who had already halved the distance between them. She pushed forward as fast as she could, using her staff for balance. Mezhik crawled across her fingers and warmed her hand.

Magus's naked form still haunted her from earlier, and she wanted nothing more than to take her rage out on the approaching man. But she remained in control. She must. Like her, the sentry might have no choice but to serve Magus.

She halted about ten feet from the man, and he did the same. He held a bow in his left hand, arrow nocked and string drawn, aimed at her chest. Her hand curled with rage as mezhik pumped through her veins.

Stave your anger. This day, he's not the enemy.

"Lower your hood," barked the man. "And don't even think about reaching for your dagger."

As though blown back by a gale-force wind, her hood slipped off the back of her head with only a thought. Terror and rage fueled her words. "You dare address me in that fashion? Do you not know who I am?"

Lightning flashed, creasing the dark sky, and a barrage of thunder rumbled close behind.

Perfect timing.

The whites of the man's eyes grew large. "Mistress Darkridge?"

"Then you do know me. Lower your weapon before I remove your arm."

The tension eased on the bow. "You shouldn't be out here."

Emorith took several steps forward, mezhik still flowing in and around her fingers. She snarled, "And who are you to say where I should or should not be?"

He held up his arm. "No, you misunderstand what I'm saying. These woods are far more dangerous than you could imagine. Why do you think King Carac brought so many soldiers?"

She had wondered just that but wrote it off as mere precaution. Magus, if anything, planned out each scenario meticulously. She drew her mezhik back. "And what makes these woods dangerous besides the terrain?"

The man looked about nervously. "Ferzh."

"Overgrown wolves?" she scoffed. "Are you toying with me?"

He shook his head. "Never, Mistress! It's the sole reason I'm out here and the reason we have so many patrols."

"I—"

Trees rustled to the west of them. They both turned, Emorith calling forth her mezhik once again and the sentry readying his bow, but they moved far too slow. A black mass larger than a man streaked over the top of the ridge, little more than a flash of darkness, dragging the sentry along as it disappeared into the trees on the other side of the ridge. He'd had no chance to cry for help.

Emorith's heart quaked in her chest. "Illian!" She turned and descended the western slope with abandon.

Lightning and thunder filled the night sky and torrential rains swept down the slope with ever-increasing flow, slickening the rocky terrain. Thrice Emorith lost her footing, scraping her knees and twisting her ankle two of those times. Had she been without her staff, she would've found herself face-down at the bottom of a ravine.

Her life held no meaning without Illian, so she pushed the falls from her mind and moved faster. The rain, lightning, and darkness kept her distracted, and she reached the bottom of the slope quicker than she thought possible.

A narrow but fast-moving river raged before her. She couldn't judge the depth in the darkness, but it made little difference as she could teleport herself across it. Had Javana and Illian made it this far before the rains began? The thought concerned her, but not as much as the blood-curdling scream that rose above the sound of the raging water, rain, and booming thunder.

Another scream filled the night, chilling her to the bone. It came from the same direction Javana and Illian would've gone. She didn't have time and didn't want to ponder if the screams were Illian's or Javana's. In a blink, Emorith moved from one side of the river to the other and then dashed through the trees.

Lightning flashed with ferocity, strobing light throughout the forest. Dizzying as it was, Emorith pushed on, stumbling several times but regaining her balance with the aid of her staff. She would not be too late.

A third scream, much louder than the first two, drew her to the left.

To her right, movement paralleled hers. A large, dark shape. Its howl pierced her ears. Then, to her left, another howl responded.

Thirty paces farther, she stumbled through the trees and into a clearing. Directly ahead, an outcropping of rocks stood a good twenty feet high. Pinned against the rocks by a wolf five times the size of any she'd ever seen were two figures. It had to be Illian and Javana, and a flash of lightning confirmed it. Javana stood with Illian at her back, holding a long stick. How she'd managed to keep the beast at bay with it puzzled her, but it didn't matter.

She stormed forward as an orange fireball formed above her palm. She started to fling it at the beast when the second one emerged from the trees. Both were close. No matter which one she chose to attack, the other would surely rip her limb from limb.

Both beasts turned their attention on her and began circling. Saliva hung from large, hinged jaws. Ferocious, yellowed fangs and sharp teeth glistened. Hackles raised, each stood taller than Emorith. Iridescent, red eyes glowed in the pale light of her undulating fireball. Growls rose from deep within their throats but neither advanced.

The difference in size and coloring between the two beasts led her to conclude that one was male and the other female.

The sentry atop the ridge had called them ferzh. As a young girl, she'd heard many tales of wizards and sorceresses using such beasts as both pets and as a means of transportation, but she'd thought them tall tales. Now, seeing that the beasts existed, she wondered if the legends were true.

One such legend spoke of a physical and spiritual bond that could be achieved between wizard and beast that linked the two together. Only one such link could exist at any given time, and only the death of the wizard or the beast could break it. She knew it was a stretch, but she was out of options.

What do I have to lose?

Emorith locked eyes with the one closest to Javana and Illian, the one she assumed to be male. Until that moment, she hadn't realized the sense of understanding they projected. Her pulse spiked as she reached out with her mind and connected with the beast.

According to the same legends, she must provide the beast with a name to seal the bond between them. Her skin prickled. One of them would attack.

"I will call you Raonull," she said in his mind.

A long ng filled her, deep into the depths of her being, but it wasn't her own. No words passed between them, but she understood *his* needs, wants, and fears. mages flashed in her mind, the story of his life: a warrior, a leader, brave to the bone. It spanned just a moment.

Raonull growled deep in his throat as he approached. Emorith pulled her mezhik back, and the fireball sank into her hand. A bitter howl rose behind her and filled the night. Emorith turned as a flash of lightning lit the dark sky. The female ferzh galloped toward Javana and Illian.

"Save them!" she screamed in her mind. Raonull turned and raced to intercept the other ferzh.

Another flash of lightning. The two beasts clashed together. Teeth and claws and fangs flashed in the night, mimicking the barrage of lightning as the rain continued to pour. Emorith drew closer, but then the violent quarrel came right at her. Grunts, growls, and yips echoed through the clearing.

A massive bolt of lightning shattered the night sky. Through the rain, beyond the bloody battle waging before her, stood Javana and Illian, transfixed by terror.

For a moment, time itself seemed to pause. Raindrops hung in the air, and the battle between the two ferzh ground to a halt, large paws with razor-sharp claws frozen mid-swipe and jaws ready to snap bone.

Emorith knew two things in that moment: Raonull would lose the fight, and her life would be forfeit. Neither mattered as long as Javana and Illian escaped.

She shouted *"run"* at Illian and Javana through her mind with such force and so much persuasion that blood seeped from their nostrils.

Time burst forward, and the battle came to a sickening conclusion as the female ferzh ripped a chunk of flesh from the underside of Raonull's neck. Raonull howled, and his pain ripped through Emorith as though it were her own.

Emorith doubled over and reached for her own throat, but she found no wound.

Lightning flashed.

The female ferzh stalked toward her.

Darkness. Thunder rumbled.

Emorith tried to enter the female ferzh's mind, but she couldn't. *A single connection,* she remembered. She struggled to call upon her mezhik.

Another flash.

Javana and Illian no longer stood against the outcropping.

Darkness and thunder.

Orange light arced between Emorith's fingers then faded.

No!

A third flash.

Razor claws arced backward.

Darkness swallowed her, and the ground trembled.

Emorith braced herself for impact, but how could she prepare for death in a moment's notice? During the years she lived among Fekɜzhn dhä Räd, she'd been forced to memorize many passages from a book they called *Ɂätūr's Holy Scriptures*, but she'd never given them credence or taken them to heart. For her, they'd held no meaning, but for some reason she could think of nothing else.

"Death is but a passing shadow; a transition into life everlasting. Have faith in Ɂätūr, heed His word, and death will lose its sting."

Several moments passed, but no claws ripped into her throat.

"What are you waiting for?" she yelled.

A fourth flash lit the clearing.

Raonull stood before her, the female ferzh trapped under his mighty paw. Blood dripped from his jaws and from the wound on his neck.

Lightning flashed again, revealing the pool of blood surrounding Raonull. The female ferzh' head, twisted unnaturally backward, remained attached only by the thick hide at the nape of her neck.

Emorith rose on shaky legs. Weakness drilled into her core—nearly pulled her to the ground. It took her a moment to realize Raonull no longer stood. She needed to figure out how to distinguish his feelings from hers, but now wasn't the time.

She knelt next to him. He groaned as images of death flashed through her mind. She sat in the blood, rain, and mud and placed his large head in her lap. Sorrow wracked her, her bond with Raonull stronger than any she'd ever experienced, save the one with Illian.

She needed to preserve her mezhik for persuading king Aervik, if necessary, but she couldn't just let Raonull suffer, could she? If he died, she thought she might too.

Gods, what should I do?

Two paths stood before her, but only one she could live with.

One problem at a time. Save Raonull and then worry about the rest.

Emorith reached deep within and called upon her mezhik once more. This time, it came.

She placed her orange-glowing hands over Raonull's wounded neck. She'd healed simple scratches and bruises before, but nothing as serious as the gaping hole in his neck.

Gods, let this work.

She closed her eyes. *"Beall ṭäzhädhär."*

Mezhik poured from her hands and into Raonull's wounds, orange tendrils of light that both burned and soothed. She lost track of how long she poured her mezhik into him, but she knew if she continued much longer it would kill her.

Emorith withdrew her mezhik and collapsed on top of Raonull. His mighty chest rose and fell underneath her head, but she didn't know if he'd survive. She lived because of him, and she would never forget that.

But did I do enough to save his life?

She didn't have time to think about it. She needed to get moving again before the day swallowed the night, otherwise all would be lost. She sat up and pushed Raonull's head off her lap. He didn't stir.

Emorith pulled herself to her feet, turned to locate her staff, and collapsed to her hands and knees. Her head swam and nausea gripped her stomach. She bent over and purged what remained of the boar's meat.

She coughed and spat stomach acid on the ground. She wouldn't get far in her current state and couldn't afford to rest. She needed energy to replenish what she'd poured into Raonull, and even though the thought sickened her, she had a ripe source at her disposal.

She crawled over to the dead ferzh. Flashes of lightning confirmed what she thought she'd find: blood no longer flowed from the wound. She closed her eyes and dug her fingers into the soft tissues inside the beast's torn neck. The squishing sound gagged her and sent her into a fit of dry heaving. Somehow, she regained control of herself and focused her mind on the task. Illian's life still depended on her.

Emorith scraped out what she could with her nails and shoved the small mass of blood and tissue into her mouth before she had a chance to rethink it. The repulsive taste took her to the edge of vomiting once again, and swallowing it down took every ounce of willpower she could muster. She repeated the process twice more before her strength began to return.

She took a deep breath, stilling her trembling hands. Her heart fought against her mind, begging her to make do with the strength she'd gained, but she knew what lay ahead of her would require her full strength, and she wasn't there.

One last time. For Illian.

Emorith unsheathed the dagger hanging from her belt and plunged it into the beast's stomach several times. She cut an opening through its thick skin and then she shoved her arm elbow-deep into the ferzh' stomach. The heart would provide the nutrients and energy she needed. Once she located it, she cut the arteries and veins around it with her knife, wrapped her fingers around it, and twisted and ripped it out. She sat back and sank her teeth into the large muscle, filling her mouth with the coppery taste of blood once again. Blood oozed down the sides of her mouth, but with each swallow came greater strength.

Emorith stood on solid legs and tossed the heart over to Raonull. She raised her head skyward and let the rain wash the blood from her face. Nothing would save her clothes. She wiped her dagger on her cloak and sheathed it.

She reached out to Raonull with her mind and entered his. Immediately, his fatigue weighed her down but his pain bearable. He'd survive, and it filled her with joy. *"Thank you, my friend. I'll never forget what you did for me."*

Raonull groaned, and several images flashed through her mind, but each faded before she could decipher it. She wished that she could stay with him until he fully recovered, but she had a task to complete and no one's life held more importance than Illian's did.

Emorith retrieved her staff and drew upon her mezhik. *"Əllíṭ ʊb."*

An orange ball of light rose in front of her and pushed back the night. She glanced down at Raonull one final time, and then headed toward the entrance to Intus.

† † †

Emorith rounded the last bend, hoping beyond hope that Illian and Javana would be there to greet her, but the tunnel entrance stood empty. She found no indication that they'd passed that way either, but the torrential downpour would've erased any evidence they might've left behind within minutes.

May the gods protect you, Illian. Or Ɂäṭūr if he is the true God.

The tunnel entrance stood a little more than five feet wide and seven feet tall, just large enough to accommodate a small, horse-drawn cart. The tunnel itself didn't go straight back but angled to the left and descended at a slow grade. A hundred feet in, the tunnel opened to a massive expanse more than six miles wide at its narrowest point and several thousand feet in height.

Emorith stopped, extinguished her light, and took in the majestic view.

The switchback road descended at least another thousand feet from where she stood before leveling out, but the pristine lake drew her attention again, just as it had a few nights ago.

The lake, many miles long and wide, spanned the distance between the switchback trail and the city of Intus. Luminescent, white rocks lined the lake's deep bottom, giving it unprecedented clarity and beauty. Schools of fish and other creatures filled its waters, and clumps of vibrant plants sprung up from its depths. The aethershard crystal's blue light enhanced the lake's beauty, its reflection atop the lake's calm surface reminiscent of an ethereal moon.

From where she stood, Emorith couldn't see what she knew to be true: the lake waters surrounded Intus like a moat, creating an island beneath the mountain. However, she could make out the dozens of arches that spanned the far edge of the lake. Those arches supported part of the road that circled Intus and allowed the lake waters to flow freely around the city.

The skirmish with the ferzh hurt Emorith on many fronts. Not only did it waste precious time she didn't have, but it also ruined her clothes and drained her mezhik. Granted, the ferzh blood helped replenish some of her mezhik, but she still didn't have the strength to teleport herself into the city and accomplish all that she must. She didn't know what to do about the clothes.

One problem at a time. I must get there first.

Emorith traversed the switchback road down to the cave floor, but more than ten miles still lay between her and the city gates. She prided herself on staying in decent shape, but this night proved far more brutal than she'd anticipated. Her knees ached from the many spills she took traversing the mountain, but the pain paled in comparison to what she'd suffer at the hands of Magus.

This will not be for nothing. Gods, make it so.

She huffed. "A few days, and I've come to rely on gods I don't even know."

But I'll take all the help I can get.

Emorith set forth along the narrow section of road that skirted the right-hand side of the lake. One side of the road butted up to sheer rock walls that soared toward the cave's domed ceiling far above, and the other side dropped a dozen feet and into the lake.

A few miles' walk brought her to a 'T' in the road. Straight ahead lay Intus and a severe drop-off into a wide moat that both surrounded and protected the city. To the right, the road continued to hug the rock wall as it circled the city, and to the left, the road crossed the lake on a bridge with many arches—

the one she'd seen from the top of the switchback road. Either direction led to the far side of the city and the single entrance into Intus. The difference between the two directions boiled down to two things: time and distance versus beauty.

Beauty won't save Illian or Intus.

Emorith veered to the right as time never favored her.

Two hours later, she arrived at the bridge into Intus. At five times the breadth of the road, the massive, hewn stone bridge stretched across the expanse in a single arch. Rock walls lined both sides of the bridge with just enough height to keep from plunging over it but not enough to block the view. Across the bridge stood an archway several stories tall and as wide as the bridge. Massive iron gates stood open, welcoming all into the city without sun.

A massive square sat at the center of Intus, and each of its four points dissected the city into pie-shaped chunks. The area leading into the city housed the hunters and fishermen, giving them the best access in and out of the city. Directly across the square lived the weavers, masons, and smiths who worked with precious gems, metals, fabrics, and stones to create weapons, armor, clothing, and artwork. To the right of the square were buildings dedicated to many different religions and gods. To the left, the Hall of Kings rose above all other buildings.

Emorith stuck to the shadows as she headed toward the Hall of Kings, weaving her way down several roads and avoiding the handful of dwellers skulking about. She lowered her hood and drew her cloak tight as she neared the front steps of the hall.

As with many of the buildings in Intus, rough-hewn stones—black rock with gold veins and speckled with various shades of gray—covered the entire front of the Hall of Kings, most likely quarried straight from the walls of the cavern itself.

Cylindrical, granite columns, fluted at the top and spiraled down their length with wide, square bases, held up the triangular-shaped pediment. The pediment itself featured ornate carvings, inlaid with gold, and its solid face displayed the name of the building in gold lettering: Hūəll ef Kinzhɛ.

Hall of Kings.

She ascended the fifteen black marble steps up to the hall's entrance, but the white-iron gates stood closed and locked. To the left of the gates, she eyed a bell, so she reached over and rang it. Several minutes passed without a response, so she rang it again, louder and longer.

A man approached from beyond the gate. He wore plain clothes, and little distinguished him from the other dwellers she'd encountered except for his long, bushy eyebrows.

"Hold your horses, young lady. There's no need to enact violence on the bell. It serves its purpose well."

"I must see King Aervik."

He held a hand up to his ear. "Pardon? Must've misunderstood you. Thought you said you wanted to see the king. What a silly notion at this hour." He chuckled.

She didn't have time to waste. "Take me to see King Aervik!"

He lifted a finger. "Ah, you did say that." He pulled on his ear. "Afraid you'll have to wait. King's not an early riser."

Urgency brought forth her mezhik. "You want to open the gate and let me in."

The man cocked his head. "Yes, yes. I do want to open the gate, and that requires a key..." He patted his shirt pockets and dug his hands into his trousers. "...but a key I do not have."

"Then go get it!"

"You're a feisty little thing, aren't you?" He winked at her. "I'll be back before you can say bugger bees." He disappeared from her view.

"Bugger bees," she muttered.

"Got yourself in some sort of bind?"

Emorith turned around. Tuvak leaned against one of the columns. A pipe hung from his mouth.

Relief washed over her. "Thank the gods you're here! You must get me in to see your father."

Tuvak cocked his head and eyed her. "And why would I take some stranger to see my father?"

"We met last night—"

And I told him to forget it all.

He chuckled. "Sometimes the drink gets the best of me, but I'd remember meeting a rousing woman such as you."

Emorith pulled her cloak open, revealing her blood-stained clothes. Tuvak gasped, and the pipe fell from his mouth. He fumbled for his knife, managed to free it from its sheath, and then dropped it on the ground. He bent down to retrieve it, but she reached out, and the knife flew into her hand.

Tuvak looked up, his eyes narrowed to slits. "A sorceress. Why the gods are you here?"

She pointed the knife at him. "Take me to your father!"

"Can I help you with something?"

Emorith lowered the knife and turned back to see that the old man stood at the gate again. "Did you find the keys?"

He scratched his head. "Not sure I follow. Why would I need keys?"

Had she really risked hers and Illian's life for a city full of mad people?

Perhaps I'm the one who's mad.

She turned back to Tuvak who still knelt. "What are you waiting for?"

He rose to his feet, hands held high. "Whoa, are you serious? Waking my father in the middle of the night would be the worst plan ever. You do that, and he'll never listen to you, no matter what you have to say."

"Just do it!" She seethed.

"Fine." He shook his finger at her. "I think I'm starting to remember you." He walked over to the gate and opened it with a key from his pocket. He swept his arm toward the opening. "Ladies first."

Emorith and Tuvak slipped inside the gate, and the old man shut and locked it behind them.

Tuvak chuckled. "Keep the key, Bordel. It's yours anyway."

Bordel gawked at the key, then grinned. "Ah, so it is."

Tuvak snapped his fingers. "Yeah… it's all coming back to me now. You left me on the temple steps last night, didn't you?"

"Yes, but that doesn't matter. You need to stay focused. Get us to your father as quickly as you can."

He nodded and headed into the Hall of Kings. They talked as he led her through many dark corridors.

It took all of five minutes for him to ask the question she knew he'd been wanting to ask. "So, is that your blood, or someone else's?"

"Neither. It's ferzh blood."

He stopped in the middle of the corridor, his mouth agape. "You took on a ferzh and lived to talk about it?"

"I had help." She grabbed Tuvak's arm and pushed him forward. "Come on, we need to keep moving."

They turned down another corridor and then took the third left. Two men dressed in full battle armor stood ten paces down the short hall, guarding two large doors. Both lowered their pikes.

Tuvak stopped abruptly and arm blocked Emorith. "Whoa, hold up guys. She's with me, and we're here to see my father."

The guard on the left stepped forward and bowed. "Prince Tuvak. You know the law decreed by King Aervik. No one shall disturb the king's rest, including his own sons."

Tuvak nodded. "I do, but we come with urgent news."

Emorith kept silent.

Perhaps Tuvak can work this out and save me my energy.

The guard on the right spoke up. "No news is worth losing your head, and I like mine right where it is. Come back in the morning."

Emorith pushed Tuvak aside and advanced several steps. Both guards tensed up. She released her cloak and let it fall open. Somehow, their white faces paled further.

She snarled, "Open the door, or the entire city will be dead tomorrow."

The guards held their ground. The one on the left said, "Turn around and leave, or you never will."

So, this is the way it's gonna be?

She drew upon her mezhik, and it flowed into her tongue. She opened her mouth to speak, but then the double doors swung open.

A short man, bald with four sinewy scars atop his head symbolizing a crown, stood in the doorway. A deep-purple robe hung from his shoulders, loosely drawn, but not enough to cover his bare chest and white skivvies. A small tuft of white hair hung from his lower jaw, little more than a few strands. Beyond the hair and the extra scars atop his head, his resemblance to Tuvak was uncanny. A golden chain hung from his thick neck, and a golden ring with a blue, glowing gem covered half of his right middle finger.

King Aervik.

"What the gods is going on out here?" King Aervik rubbed his eyes with his fists. "A man can't sleep in his own—" His face paled when he finally took in the scene that greeted him.

Emorith acquired her new target and laced her words with persuasion. "Your highness, you *need* to speak with me."

The guard on the right laughed. "Do you really think—"

"Silence," said King Aervik. He yawned and shook his head a bit. "I'm awake now, so she may as well speak."

Emorith took another step forward and the guards moved to block her path.

"You're as close as you're gonna get to the king," said the guard on the left.

This must end now.

Emorith smiled at the two guards and forced more mezhik into her words. "Send these men away," she said to King Aervik.

King Aervik pushed his way between the two guards. "Let the woman pass. She is my guest." His brow furrowed. "And do not disturb us."

"My king?" said the guard on the right.

King Aervik turned toward the man. "Do you question my authority?"

"Certainly not, my king." The man tripped over his own tongue.

"Good. Raise your weapons and allow her to pass." King Aervik drew his robe tight.

The two guards looked at each other and slowly raised their pikes. Emorith stepped between them and followed King Aervik into his bedchambers. She turned, closed the doors in Tuvak's face, and locked them.

King Aervik ushered her over to a plush couch covered with furs. "Please, have a seat."

She complied, and King Aervik sat down next to her, far closer than she would've liked. She held onto her staff and placed her free hand in her lap.

King Aervik placed his hand on the couch between them. "Would you like some refreshments? Some wine, perhaps?"

"No, your highness. I appreciate the thought but the news I've come to give you is of the gravest kind."

His hand slid a bit closer. "Please tell me what bothers you, and I will make it go away."

"Magus Carac, the king of the south, waits outside your city, poised to attack. You must defend the city."

King Aervik's hand touched the side of her leg, and his lips curled into a smile. She willed herself to refrain from slapping it away. "As I'm sure you know, we are peaceful people. Hence the reason I have so few guards. We've never taken up arms against another kingdom, nor have we ever needed to."

His arrogance rivaled that of Magus. Emorith gripped her staff tighter. "If you don't, you'll be slaughtered like pigs."

His hand crawled up the side of her thigh and rested atop it. "You misunderstand my meaning. We have certain defenses that protect our city from attacks when the need arises. However, we've not used them in a millennium." He cocked his head. "How could I be certain you're telling me the truth?"

She pushed his hand away and rose from the couch. "Don't you see? I'm with those who have come to destroy you."

He smiled and stood. "If what you say is true, why are you warning me?"

"I've befriended your son, Eshtak." She sighed. "Look, I can't stand the thought of anything bad happening to your people and your city. Magus will kill every last one of you."

King Aervik sat back down on the couch and rested his head in his hands. He jerked with sobs.

Rage swelled in Emorith. She drew upon her mezhik once again. Through gritted teeth, she said, "Get off the godforsaken couch and get your priest to raise the barrier!"

He looked up at her. Tears streamed down his cheeks. "There's nothing

I want more than to do what you ask of me, but it isn't possible."

"Not possible?" His words caught Emorith off-guard. "What's that supposed to mean?"

He hung his head. "I… I'm so ashamed."

"There's no time to waste." She pushed him again with persuasion. "Tell me the problem so that I can help you fix it."

"We have no priest." King Aervik shook his head. "Three generations have passed since our last priest died."

Emorith had to sit down, the revelation too shocking.

Maybe these people do deserve to die.

"How do you face your people each day knowing that an attack would wipe you out?"

"I didn't think it would ever happen. Besides, how would we go about finding a replacement?"

She hated to admit it, but he posed a good question. A query such as that would itself bring about their demise. Maybe lying about their defenses had been the only play they had.

Her stomach turned.

Magus must've found out about this.

She still had a card to play. She rose from the couch. "Take me to the temple and show me what must be done. I'll raise the barrier myself."

"You? And how would a beautiful young woman such as yourself do that?"

She thrust her hand toward him. Orange flames rose from her palm. "All of us hold secrets."

King Aervik recoiled. "By the gods…"

Emorith extinguished the flames and leaned on her staff. "Magus has dozens of people like me. Your city will melt into the lake if we don't act now."

King Aervik nodded. "I will show you the temple. May *Eallizenōz*, our stone god, help you raise the barrier." He rose from the couch.

"Good. How long will it take?"

He shrugged and urged her to follow him. "From the knowledge passed down through the ages, maybe ten minutes. No more than that."

They crossed the room and headed through the doors. Tuvak still stood in the hall.

"And how far does the barrier extend?" she asked.

King Aervik spoke as they walked through the Hall of Kings. "I believe it stops at the road, but none of us have ever seen it."

Tuvak followed them. "Where are we headed?"

"The temple," said Emorith. "I'm going to raise the barrier."

"But that's the priest's job," argued Tuvak.

King Aervik stopped in the corridor for a moment and addressed Tuvak. "We have no priest, son. Emorith is our last hope. And the temple only serves as a symbol. We're headed to the crystal room."

Tuvak's mouth gaped upon hearing King Aervik's statement. King Aervik dismissed him with the flick of his wrist. "One day, you will know everything, my son."

King Aervik turned and led them down another corridor to a dead end. A massive, rectangular stone with an aethershard crystal engraved on its front hugged the wall. He pressed on the crystal with his palm, waited several seconds, and then stepped back. The stone scraped against the floor and rumbled as it arced outward, revealing a hidden tunnel.

Once inside, Emorith realized they entered a labyrinth of tunnels designed to hide the way to the actual crystal room. White stones, the same as those that lined the bottom of the lake, lined the walls in regular intervals, each providing just enough light to see the path between it and the next stone. King Aervik didn't hesitate once as he led them through a multitude of passages, twisting and turning them toward a destination she couldn't imagine.

Finally, they entered a square room. A large, altar-shaped stone sat at its center. A book lay open atop it.

King Aervik nodded toward the stone. "Do what needs done."

After everything she'd learned, it didn't surprise her that he had no further knowledge as to how to raise the barrier. She walked over to the stone and read the instructions written in Ancient Centaurian.

Three steps. Simple enough.

She turned to Tuvak and King Aervik. "There are two hidden pockets in the outer walls, one on either side of the stone. Locate them and place one hand in each of them at the same time. Whatever happens, do not remove your hands."

They both set to work, each taking a side. Tuvak located his first and King Aervik found his soon after. They looked at each other, nodded, and each shoved a hand into the wall. Both men yelped at the same time. Emorith snickered, their yelps nearly identical.

The ceiling above them quaked, raining dust down on everything. The ceiling slid back in four separate sections. Emorith looked up as the dust settled. The room they stood in sat directly beneath the aethershard crystal.

"Remove your hands," she said.

They did. Each dripped with blood. The floor of the room quaked, just as the ceiling had, and the floor rose until it became level with the surrounding center square of Intus.

"Gods…" said Tuvak and King Aervik in unison.

Emorith withdrew her dagger and slid it across her scarred palm. She squeezed her hand and let the blood drip onto the book she read from. Smoke rose from the pages and the book turned to ash. With her fingertip, she drew a rune that matched the aethershard crystal.

"Protect," she said and backed away from the large stone.

The stone fissured and then its outer surface exploded into a cloud of dust. When the dust cleared, Emorith finally understood how the barrier worked. Beneath the stone altar's surface sat another aethershard crystal, this one red.

Beams of red light shot upward and streamed into the blue aethershard crystal above it. The blue light of Äfärəlleʐʈinzh began turning purple. She, Tuvak, and King Aervik gathered a good distance from the crystal.

Emorith's legs grew weary, so she leaned heavily on her staff. She couldn't use much more mezhik without trapping herself in Intus as well.

A loud horn moaned, filling the cavern with woeful echoes.

King Aervik looked up toward the Hall of Kings. "That would be the warning for all to return before the barrier rises."

She nodded. "Good. I must leave before I lose my chance."

King Aervik took her hand and kissed the top of it. "We are indebted to you, but how will we turn it back off once the threat is gone?"

"It may take some time, but I'll return when it's safe. How much food do you have?"

King Aervik's expression turned grim. "A few months. Perhaps three. We should've been more prepared."

"I'll make it work." She looked up at Äfärǝlleʑţinzh. "Now, I must go."

He let go of her hand. "I understand."

Emorith stepped back and teleported out of the city square and onto the road beyond the bridge leading into Intus. She crumpled to the ground, her body drained to its limit.

Several dwellers emerged from the night and quickly crossed the bridge. One woman offered her a hand, but Emorith shooed her away. The aethershard crystal brightened, a light that rivaled the sun, and a purple circle grew and arced over the city and plunged into the depths of the surrounding moat, creating a bubble around the entire island.

Thank the gods.

So focused on the barrier, she started when she heard movement to her left. Had some of the dwellers not made it back in time? She lacked the energy to turn her head.

A hand grabbed her by her hair and yanked her head back. Magus leered down at her. "Hello, Emorith."

CHAPTER SIX

Emorith couldn't figure out how Magus had arrived so quickly, but it made no difference. The barrier stood and Intus would survive. Now, she needed to fight for her life so she could get back to Illian.

Magus knew nothing of Emorith's treachery yet, and with the right words, he might never know the truth. She searched her mind for the perfect lie, but her current state clouded her mind.

Magus snarled, "What have you done?"

Emorith gazed into his rage-filled eyes. "Magus... I tried to stop them from raising the barrier, but I didn't have the strength."

Magus lowered her head and knelt on one knee. "Did you?" She nodded. "And why did you come here on your own?"

Words spilled from her mouth, and she prayed they sounded convincing. "When I came here a few nights ago, I heard people talking about seeing an army in the valley. I knew word would eventually make it to King Aervik's ears and he would act upon the threat. I didn't know the city had a barrier until it was too late. I barely made it out before it closed off the city."

"Yes, of course. But why didn't you come to me with this news days ago when you returned with the test subject?"

"You saw the state I was in. I didn't remember until last night, so I acted upon it. Forgive me, my liege."

Magus pushed a rogue strand of hair from Emorith's face. Him touching anything of hers sickened her, but it paled in comparison to the look in his eyes. "Ah, my Emmy." The only times Magus called her that came right before he turned violent. "Listen to yourself. Do you believe your own lies?" He grabbed her by the throat and shoved her against the wall. "You were not incapacitated until after the protection spell was cast on the test subject."

Emorith froze. How could she have said something so stupid? The thought of begging Magus to spare her life flitted through her mind, but she'd never forgive herself if she did, and it would do her no good. No one crossed Magus and lived.

A streak of defiance rose within her. "You're right. I betrayed you, and I've never felt so good."

The left side of Magus's mouth curled upward. "And it was worth the life of our son?"

"I've ensured you'll never lay a finger on him!"

"I concede. He's beyond my reach now, but death will soon find him."

She groaned. "And what's that supposed to mean?"

He looked toward the gates of Intus. "I see the boy now."

Her pulse spiked. "That's impossible."

Magus reached down and lifted her into a sitting position. "Tell me what you see."

Emorith gazed across the bridge and to the massive city gates, but her eyes blurred with fatigue. She blinked several times and squinted, and the world came back into focus. Two figures stood in front of the left gate.

"Illian!"

Fear strangled her, and her vision shook with each violent heartbeat as the blood drained from her face. She tried to stand but didn't have the strength. Illian's arms stretched toward her, but Javana held him firmly around the waist. It didn't make sense.

Why are they here and not a day closer to Duos Flumen?

Her head spun and her stomach churned. "At least he's safe from you!"

Magus laughed. "Yes, but not from scourge."

No, it's not possible!

"The barrier will protect them." She sounded desperate even to herself.

"No, Emmy, the barrier will protect us."

"What?" Her thoughts raged beyond control.

He stroked her hair. "You're nothing, if not predictable. I knew from the day we met that you'd eventually betray me, so I worked it into my campaign from the beginning.

"You pretend that you only care for Illian, but your heart has always been weak. I saw the way you and Illian latched onto that vile creature as though it were worthy of more than death. You disgust me."

She spat at him, but it only dribbled on her chin. "It's mutual."

"Good." Magus grabbed a handful of her hair and yanked her head back. "The next time I use you, I'll bash your head in, but I'll only heal you enough to keep you alive. By the time you die, you'll be so deformed that no one will recognize you."

She needed to find some way to save Illian, but her thoughts wouldn't stay straight in her head.

"You're not going to kill me?"

"And let you miss watching your son die? Never."

"You still haven't explained how you plan on conjuring scourge with the barrier up. And even if you manage to get them to lower it, I'll never help you again."

Magus sighed. "You are far denser than I could have ever imagined. As I told you, every aspect of my campaign hinged on your actions. You assumed that meant I needed you to help conjure all the spells. Only the first required your assistance, and you did well.

"I chose you to find a test subject not because of your persuasion skills but because of your vile compassion. I knew that if I sent you into Intus you would be unable to finish what we started. You thought you could hide our son from me and thwart me by refusing to cooperate. Did you really think it so simple?"

"How did you find Javana and Illian?"

Magus shook with laughter. "One need not find what isn't lost."

Emorith's eyes widened. "Javana..."

He nodded. "That's right. Javana betrayed your trust."

"When she slept with you..."

How could I have been so careless?

"Is that what she told you?" He laughed again. "She's a devious liar… and my sister."

Sister?

Had she not handpicked the woman herself to watch over Illian? She was the one who manipulated people, so how did Magus manipulate her so well?

"But what of the barrier? How could you have planned for that?"

"As I said, you're predictable. You played right into my hand every step of the way. No containment spell would've ever worked to contain scourge. A thousand wizards wouldn't have the strength to hold it back."

He gazed upward. "However, the aethershard crystals contain more power than all the wizards who have ever lived combined. Their protective barrier is the only thing that could contain scourge. We needed the barrier activated so that scourge could be cast." He kissed her forehead. "Thank you for persuading King Aervik to do what was necessary."

"But… your sister's in there. She'll die."

Magus shrugged. "A necessary sacrifice. Besides, she's *ʊnzhiftäd*, just like Illian. No place exists in this world for those like them."

One of Magus's soldiers approached and bowed. "My liege, the wizards and sorceresses are in position around the city."

"Good. Take the test subject and cast him through the barrier."

"Yes, my liege."

Magus rose. "Twenty minutes, and the campaign will come to fruition." He pulled Emorith to her feet, but her numb legs were far too weak to hold her up. "You are pathetic."

Magus released her arm and she crumpled to the ground. How had he found favor with the gods when she hadn't?

They're as vengeful as he is.

Nothing mattered anymore. She had no strength to lift her head. Illian would die a few hundred feet away and she was powerless to stop it. Hope failed her. The gods failed her. She failed Illian.

When the wizards and sorceresses conjured scourge, she'd use the last bit of her mezhik and die with Illian and the people of Intus. It was the only thing left she had control of. Magus would never use her again.

A silver ring dropped in front of her face.

Żäbräżär…

The collar, a seamless piece of silver metal forged with dragon's fire and imbued with mezhik, had but one use: to suppress and capture the mezhik of its wearer. The mezhik it captured could then be harvested by another wizard or sorceress. To the free world, its usage spoke of slavery and garnered deep hatred, but for Magus, it furthered his plans.

A lump rose in Emorith's throat.

Does Magus know my final plan?

"The collar contains enough mezhik to get you on your feet again but not enough for you to run. Use it and watch our son die with dignity."

Have the gods not failed me after all?

She slid her hand over to the collar and pulled its stored mezhik into herself. Feeling returned to her legs, and with it, strength. She pushed herself into a sitting position.

Two soldiers dragged Eshtak over to the bridge where the barrier rose up through it. They dragged him through the barrier and dropped him on the bridge. A moment later, the two soldiers exploded into plumes of ash. Eshtak remained unscathed but lay unconscious.

Emorith's stomach gurgled. Would the protection spell save him from scourge as well? She prayed it wouldn't but feared the worst.

Magus folded his arms, a smug grin on his face. "Not long now." He walked over to one of the wizards.

Emorith's staff lay several feet away. With it, she'd have the strength to do a little more than just stand. She reached out and her staff slid across the granite slab. Magus turned back just as she wrapped her hand around the staff. She absorbed the small amount of mezhik she'd stored within it just before Magus ripped it from her grasp.

"Did you think I wouldn't notice?"

It didn't matter. She got what she needed from it.

Emorith looked past Magus. A third figure stood close to Javana and Illian. She squinted.

Tuvak!

She drew upon her power of persuasion and spoke directly into Tuvak's mind with her own. *"Save my son! Take him to the temple and to the mirror."* Blood dripped from her nostrils, but she pushed harder, sending images of the passage and the chamber behind the temple into his mind as well.

Then, with every last ounce of mezhik she possessed, she spoke to Illian with her mind. *"I love you, my son. Go with the man. Think of home at the mirror. Hide from everyone. Find Saskia."*

Gods, I hope he passes through the mirror unharmed.

Something flashed in her peripheral vision and then the left side of her head exploded with pain. Darkness swept in and pulled her into its arms.

† † †

Emorith roused from sleep. A bright blue light stung her eyes when she opened them. Her head pulsed with pain and her left ear rang. She tried to move but her body refused to respond.

For a moment, she remembered nothing, but then her memories came flooding back, drowning her with shame and sorrow.

Illian!

A man stood over her. Young face. Armor covered his shoulders. "She's awake, my liege."

"Move her over here and lean her against the wall so she can watch."

The man grabbed her by the ankles and dragged her across the granite slabs. He grabbed her right arm and yanked her upright. Magus stood next to her.

"You managed to have Javana killed, but I fail to see the point. She would have died once the scourge spell was cast anyway. However, it does give me hope that you're salvageable. We are similar, you know."

Across the bridge, Javana lay face-down with a knife in her back. She would've given anything for it to have been Magus lying there. "I'm nothing like you. She may have betrayed me, but I never wanted her to suffer for it. Her death is on your hands."

"Is it? None of this would've been possible without your power of persuasion. So, as I see it, all their deaths will be on your hands. Tens of thousands. You're ruth—"

The entire mountain quaked as dozens of mezhik streams blasted the aethershard crystal. The crystal grew darker, its purple glow slowly shifting to black. Emorith couldn't just sit there and watch Magus destroy an entire civilization. She must act.

She didn't have the strength to persuade all the wizards and sorceresses to stop. She didn't think she had the strength to persuade even one of them, but she had to try. She dug deep and called upon her mezhik, but nothing happened. She tried again, to no avail. She couldn't even touch her mezhik. The feeling hearkened back to life before her sixteenth birthday—before her mezhik had awakened.

Her mind rolled back a few dozen minutes into the past, and her hand shot to her neck. A seamless collar circled her neck.

Ɛäbräɛär.

Magus glared down at her. "Do you think I'm foolish enough to allow you to try something again?"

"You are a fool if you let me live. Mark my words, if you don't kill me this day, I'll find a way to drive a stake through your cold heart."

"A challenge? I accept. Killing you would be far too easy..." He rubbed his hands together. "Scourge has been released!"

Emorith looked up at the crystal. A black smoke or fog poured out from the bottom of it and started filling the space inside the barrier. Within minutes, the swirling darkness descended toward the tallest buildings. Cries of terror rose from the city, and many of the dwellers poured through the city gates and crossed the bridge. Nearly a hundred of them breached the barrier and burst into ash before the others realized they couldn't escape.

They screamed and pleaded to be released, but the darkness continued to descend and consume the city. The screams grew louder—shrill shrieks that penetrated Emorith's ears even as she covered them. Never had she heard such utter terror. Another minute, and the entire city fell under the shroud of darkness. The screams became less frequent.

One dweller remained alive, his back to the barrier. Emorith watched in horror as hands reached out of the darkness and separated the man from his soul. His scream she'd never forget.

"Now we wait," Magus said.

The barrier shuddered and then expanded all the way out to the circular road and consumed the dozens of wizards and sorceresses surrounding it. Their screams lasted no more than a moment.

"That shouldn't have happened," said Magus, concern in his voice.

The barrier shuddered again and expanded toward Emorith and Magus. Black, shadowy arms stretched from the darkness, fingers clawing at them.

Emorith closed her eyes.

This is the end.

As long as Illian made it to the mirror and passed through it without turning to ash, she could live with death. She breathed slowly and prayed Illian had.

I know he's zhiftäd.

A hand grabbed her ankle.

† † †

A burst of light flashed through Emorith's eyelids and then death settled over her, a blanket of darkness. She awaited the black, clawed hands to pull her into the tempest, rip her soul from her body, and drag her into the world between life and death—the between. Several minutes passed, but the pain never roused.

She opened her eyes, but darkness remained with her. A cold, firm surface pressed against her right side, and sharp rocks poked her knees and forearms. Her first thought was to roll onto her back, but if she lay between the wall and the barrier she might roll right into death.

With the collar around her neck, she'd never be able to use her mezhik. Without mezhik, she'd never escape. She feared death, but what choice did she have? She couldn't lie there forever.

Face your fear.

She rolled onto her back, yet she still lived. Then, as her eyes adjusted to the darkness, she noticed faint white lights to her left. She rolled again, onto her left side, and stared into the deep, clear lake.

Somehow, she'd managed to move from the road in front of the bridge leading into Intus all the way around the city and close to the switchback road that led out of Intus.

She tried to sit up, but it required far more energy than she possessed. Her head proved difficult to hold up as well, but she managed a glance farther up the granite slab road. A body lay on the ground. Silver strands of hair.

Magus! What the gods happened?

A low groan forced her head off the ground once more. Magus stirred.

She would've gladly forfeited her life if it took his as well, but none of the gods favored her, not even Ɂäṭūr. She turned her head back toward the lake. In the distance, where Intus and the bridge with many arches once drew the eye, lurked death. Far above Intus, where the blue light of Äfärəlleʑṭinzh had shone so bright, nothing remained but darkness.

A reflection of my soul.

In a way, Magus had been right. Every person in Intus lay dead because of her. Not by her hand, but because she'd betrayed what she knew to be right to save her son. Had she the chance to go back and do things over, would she have the strength to make different choices? She didn't know.

Yesterday, the answer had been so simple. Her love for Illian exceeded all things, and nothing else in existence could take his place in her heart. Given any choice, his life would always come first. But now, knowing what she allowed—no, caused—to happen, could she really choose to destroy an entire race?

Perhaps Magus was right. Maybe I'm more like him than I want to admit.

Magus grunted. "Are you still alive?"

"I am, no thanks to you."

"I'm the only reason you're not in the between right now." Anger flared in his voice. "I risked my life to save you."

"Save me?" Never had Emorith known someone so pompous and arrogant. Her hands curled into fists, and she craved punching his face. "And how do you think you accomplished that?"

"I teleported you away from the barrier."

Emorith forced herself around to where she could see Magus. "That's impossible."

"And yet you live." Magus grunted again as he sat up. He rubbed the back of his neck. "You have so little faith."

"Faith can't accomplish the impossible."

A young soldier came running up. "My liege! I came as quickly as I could." The soldier offered Magus his hand.

Magus waved the man off and rose to his feet. "Nothing's impossible unless you make it that way. Your capacity for accomplishing great feats is only limited by your mind."

"And your strength," she said. "Teleportation takes a significant amount of mezhik and energy to accomplish. Your mezhik is formidable, but your power has limits, just as mine does. We're a good ten miles from the bridge into Intus. Teleporting yourself that far is easy enough but teleporting two people even a mile increases the required mezhik a hundredfold. No one can teleport two people a thousand miles."

"For most, that is true." Magus walked over and stood over her. His lips curled into the most vile and wicked grin she'd ever witnessed. "Embrace the darkness as I have, and those limits will be shattered."

Emorith didn't understand what darkness had to do with power. "Explain what you mean."

"Mezhik derk. Allow me to demonstrate it for you." Magus turned and motioned the young soldier forward.

"My liege?" The soldier bowed. "How may I serve you?"

Magus eyed the man. "What is your name?"

"Garrik, my liege."

"Tell me the purpose of your life, Garrik."

Garrik cleared his throat. "I live to serve you, my liege."

"Even unto death?" asked Magus.

Garrik nodded. "My life is yours. If you require my life, then I will gladly give it. Nothing would bring greater honor to my family."

Magus bent down next to Emorith and placed his hand on her chest.

Emorith's eyes widened, and she stiffened. "What are you doing?"

"Relax, Emorith. I'm about to show you the power of mezhik derk. In a moment, you will understand something that few do. An ancient secret so dark that its knowledge was stripped from all literature."

"Then how do you know of it?"

His eyes narrowed. "A dragon told me."

"A dragon?" she scoffed.

Emorith knew of their existence, but they were a fierce, sentient race that kept to themselves and killed anyone foolish enough to enter their domain. Few lived to tell of their encounter with one.

She rolled her eyes. "Almighty Magus, show me your dark power."

"In a moment, you'll believe." Magus growled, "Kneel, Garrik."

Garrik knelt. "What can I do?"

Magus took Garrik's hand. Garrik's eyes grew wide, but he said nothing.

Plumes of black smoke rose from each of Magus's hands and then black tendrils of mezhik wrapped his hands, covered Garrik's hand, and burned Emorith's chest. Her back arched as mezhik flowed into her.

Strength began returning to her fatigued muscles. She didn't understand how Magus could accomplish what he was doing until she looked at Garrik. Just a minute before, the young soldier had sported bright blue eyes and a plump and round face, but now, dull, grey eyes sank into dark sockets, and his cheeks turned gaunt, his face reduced to little more than flesh stretched over bone.

Emorith cried out, but her voice remained within her mind. She couldn't move or breathe. She watched in horror as Garrik's skin darkened, cracked, and peeled back, exposing bone. A few moments later, his bones turned to dust and his armor and clothes dropped into a heap on the ground.

Magus withdrew his hand from her chest, and she gasped. She sat up and dry heaved. Never had she experienced anything so wretched. She hadn't thought anything could blacken her soul further, but she'd been wrong. Even worse, Magus's power exceeded anything she thought possible. How would she ever kill a man like him?

Malice filled Magus's eyes, and through them she knew who he served: Diäfär. How could she possibly serve the same demon as Magus and stand against him? The answer required no reflection on her part.

I can't.

In that moment, she realized a truth she'd been denying her entire life: Kinzhdm ef Häfn and Ef Demd Dhä existed, literal Heaven and Hell. Because of that realization, she must make a choice. Would she continue down the path of darkness and serve the dark one himself, Diȥäfär, or would she turn to the light and serve the one true God, Ɂäṭūr?

With everything she'd seen and done over the past decade, and especially the last few days, the choice became clear. Even though she couldn't pinpoint the exact moment, her heart had changed. She didn't know how, but she'd turn from Magus and Diȥäfär and embrace Ɂäṭūr.

No matter what.

Emorith pulled herself to her feet and stared across the lake. Just hours before, its majesty had consumed her. Now, she began to see the level of destruction she'd caused. The luminescent white rocks dimmed as the waters darkened with death. Fish and other sea life floated to its surface, bloated and dead.

Death approaches.

Magus stood and grabbed her arm. "We need to leave."

She didn't fight him, but a single question niggled in her mind. She peered into his yellow eyes. "Why did you save me?"

His left nostril and the corner of his mouth rose and quivered. "To make you suffer."

Light faded from the lake, casting them into the shadows of darkness. Emorith's vision tremored, a strong gust billowed her cloak, and then she stood outside the tunnel entrance into Intus. Night had already fallen once again.

An old prophet and scribe named Kordel greeted Magus. "Success, my liege?"

Magus glared at Kordel. "That is yet to be determined."

Kordel looked past them, toward the tunnel entrance. "And the others? Are they on their way out?"

"Scourge expanded the barrier far beyond expectations. The others are all dead."

Emorith looked around. A dozen or so soldiers surrounded them. Most of them held torches with yellow flames that licked the cool, night air and plumed black smoke. The smell of burning pitch permeated the air.

Is this all that remains of the 500?

"Ah, yes. I feared as much," said Kordel. "It seems that *Äfäralleztinzh* is far more powerful than we imagined."

Magus nodded. "To say the least. Because of its power, scourge may never die out."

"And what of the test subject?"

"We may not know for some time, but I'm certain it will emerge soon if it lived. No other exit exists, and its food supply has been destroyed by scourge. You will remain here until it emerges from the tunnel."

Kordel dipped his head. "As you wish, my liege."

"Once it does emerge, kill it, and then seal the entrance. We cannot allow anyone to discover what happened here."

Kordel dipped his head again.

Magus extracted a book from within the folds of his robes and handed it to Kordel. "Daily reports."

Emorith didn't get a good look at the book, but she knew its purpose. A single page, imbued with mezhik, allowed messages to be written on it. Those messages would then be transferred to another book with its own page imbued with mezhik and linked to the first one. In this manner, messages could be passed in both directions. Such mezhik confounded her.

Magus shoved Emorith toward two soldiers that weren't holding torches. "Shackle her and take her to the ship. We set sail in an hour."

"Yes, my liege," the soldiers said in unison. One of them grabbed her arms and the other fetched a pair of ankle and wrist shackles.

A deep hatred for the soldiers holding her swelled in her chest, but it wasn't her own. She looked toward the tree line to her right. Red eyes glowed in the shadows.

Raonull.

The odds of escape stacked against Emorith. Scenarios raced through her mind, but each outcome ended in the death of her, Raonull, or them both. Two against twenty didn't make for good odds, especially with ʒäbräʒär around her neck and Magus as one of the opponents.

She connected with Raonull's mind, and a tidal wave of hatred surged into her, filling her to the point that she could hardly think or breathe. Images of death and dismemberment bombarded her and whet her appetite for blood.

She called upon the name of ʒäṭür and gained control of herself. She spoke to Raonull, *"This isn't the time, my friend. I cannot allow your death to be on my hands. I will find another way to escape."*

Anger burst from her lips in a deep, guttural growl. The two soldiers holding her arms gasped and flinched, but they didn't let go. The urge to rip their throats out and spill their blood nearly consumed her again, but she fought it.

"Leave me, Raonull. Save yourself," she said to him. *"One day I may need your strength to finish this fight, but this isn't that day."*

The two soldiers pulled her forward down the dirt road. She glanced back toward the tree line one final time but couldn't locate Raonull's red eyes. His presence slowly faded from her mind, leaving her far emptier than she thought possible.

† † †

The first week at sea, shackled and strung up below deck, wore Emorith down both mentally and physically. They afforded her a single tin of water twice a day and a small chunk of stale bread each evening. No one visited her but the burly soldier who delivered the water and bread to her. She tried talking to him the first few days, but he never said a word to her. Nor did he ever look her in the eye.

She spent most of her time fluctuating between rage and despair, calling upon and cursing the name of Ɂäʈūr, sometimes in a single breath. If she'd only been closer to the barrier. It could've saved her from thinking about Illian and wondering if he'd made it to the mirror and survived going through it.

But she didn't seek death. She'd made a promise to kill Magus, and that, coupled with her hope of Illian's survival, fueled her.

Nightmares haunted her, even as her eyes remained open. Black fingers of death reached out for her, grabbed her, and dragged her into the depths of darkness, tearing at her soul. And the wails and screams, the gnashing of teeth, filled her ears and mind.

Madness overwhelmed her, Magus the victor.

By the end of the second week, she'd all but lost the will to fight physically. However, her mind clung to grey eyes and a future she never dreamt possible. She promised herself that when Magus lay dead at her feet, she'd spend the rest of her life searching for a spectre.

Ansgar, if you're still alive, I'll find you.

A day later, they made landfall in Desolo Urbs. When the soldiers brought her up from the bowels of the ship, even the moonlight stung her eyes. She recoiled and hissed like a serpent.

She spent the next four days chained to the back of a wagon as they crossed the plains between Desolo Urbs and Galondu Castle. The sun brought back some of the sanity she'd lost on the ship, but her thoughts still remained a bit off.

When the black walls of Galondu Castle rose in the distance, her heart fluttered. The confines within its walls had served as her home for the last ten years, and it had always felt like home, even as she grew to loathe Magus. But how would she adapt without Illian? How could she live trapped inside its dungeons?

† † †

Nine weeks later, Magus came to visit Emorith in the dungeons for the first time. She hadn't seen him since the night outside the tunnel into Intus. Wrinkles crept around his eyes and lined his forehead, and his eyelids drooped over bloodshot eyes.

He's aged.

The thought satisfied her. She approached the cell bars and held onto them, but she didn't speak. In all honesty, she wasn't sure she remembered how.

He drew near. His eyes searched hers, and then his gaze traveled the length of her slender body. When his gaze met hers again, he spoke. "You've lost your curves. And your appeal."

Anger rose in her throat, but she swallowed it back down. It wouldn't serve any purpose. She found her voice, albeit a far weaker one than she remembered. "Nothing to eat or drink but bread and water has that effect."

"I've given you three months to think about your future." He clasped his hands together. "Have you come to understand that your betrayal served no purpose but to harm yourself and kill your son?"

Her heart sank. "So, scourge worked?"

Magus scowled. "On the contrary. That little *thing* never emerged."

"Then your quest to rule Centauria died with Eshtak." She forced a straight face, but joy filled her heart.

"Scourge was but one avenue. Trust me when I say that the war is coming, and there will be no stopping me once I've obtained what I need."

"And why visit me now? What is it you want from me?"

"I could still use you, Emorith. Swear your allegiance to me, and I will free you from this dungeon cell."

"That's it? A simple oath frees me?"

"I made several mistakes in the past, but I've always learned from them. I will require more than a simple oath. A blood oath."

Mix my blood with his and lock our fates together?

The idea repulsed her. She backed away from the cell bars and Magus. "You killed my son! I'll never align myself with you again."

"I had a feeling you might say that. I'm sure three more months will bring you around. I have faith in you."

He turned to leave and Emorith charged the cell bars. She grabbed them and shook them. "I hate you! My mind will never change."

Magus looked over his shoulder and grinned. "Such passion, including hate, stems from a deep love. See you soon."

With another step, Magus vanished, taking the air from the room with him. Emorith slumped to the floor, her heart full of rage, her chest full of pain, and her eyes brimming with tears. How would she ever escape? She had no one left in the world who knew she still lived.

Two months later, Emorith lay in the shadows, her mind focused on the past. She couldn't help but obsess over the man in the mirror. Strong build. Grey eyes. It had to have been Ansgar, but she couldn't figure out how he lived or why he hadn't sought her out.

Why did you leave me?

One particular teaching from Fekᴈzhn dhä Räd crawled into her mind: *"Ɂäʈūr works in mysterious ways. Sometimes we cannot comprehend the pain we must endure to bring about the greater good."*

No greater good came of any of it.

With that thought came deep conviction to the contrary.

Illian.

Her palms broke out in a sweat, and her pulse rose. Had Ansgar not left her life, she never would've met Magus and Illian would never have been born.

How did killing an entire race serve the greater good though? She couldn't come up with an answer that made sense, yet every doubt she harbored about Illian's fate vanished.

I know he lives!

She closed her eyes and prayed.

Thank you, Ɂäʈūr. I've been so focused on all the evil that I've done in the name of love that I couldn't see the good things that you've done despite me. Forgive me of my ignorance and guide my life. Show me what I must do.

Dust rained down on her face. Emorith sat up and coughed, and then she sneezed so violently that she almost smacked her head into the wall. She wiped her face on her sleeve and spat on the floor.

"What the gods was that?" Guilt rose in her throat.

I must stop saying that.

Inspection of the wall and ceiling over and around her bed rendered no results. The dust manifested from nowhere. She lay back down and stared at the wall.

Just as she started to get up to use the chamber pot, she thought she spotted one of the bricks at the head of her bed move ever so slightly. She waited several moments, forcing her eyes to keep from blinking, but it didn't move again.

I've been in here far too long.

She lifted her dress and squatted over the chamber pot but kept an eye on the brick she knew hadn't moved. Then it did again. She froze. Her heart thundered. Several more moments, but no more movement. She finished her business and stood.

The brick slid from the wall and crashed onto the bed. She yelped and quickly covered her mouth. Had she been asleep, her head would've been crushed.

She moved forward with caution and peered through the six-inch by ten-inch hole. Two green eyes glowed in the darkness.

"Eshtak comes for friend."

† † †

Eshtak pulled three more bricks out of the wall, creating a hole big enough for Emorith to squeeze through. As soon as she did, she wrapped her arms around Eshtak's neck and held onto him for several moments.

She pulled back and kissed his forehead. "How did you escape from Intus?"

"Eshtak uses mirror."

"The one behind the temple?" Eshtak nodded. "But that should've killed you."

He shrugged. "Eshtak lives."

"Yes, you do." She looked around, but the only light came through the hole from her cell. "How do we get out of here?"

"Eshtak fix wall."

Emorith nodded. Five months in confinement had clouded her head.

Eshtak jumped through the hole, shoved the brick back through it that had fallen on the bed, and then crawled back out. He carefully placed the bricks back in their place. At a glance, no one would see the cracks between the bricks, especially from the cell side since this side of the wall produced no light to filter into the cracks.

Eshtak took her hand. "Show friend outside. Must be quiet. Voices in walls hear things."

"Is that how you found me?" she whispered.

Eshtak pulled on her arm and dragged her through the dark passage. "Eshtak hears bad bad man. Bad bad man not like friend."

"I don't like him, either."

Several times as they traversed the passage, Eshtak told her to duck or step over something, so she did. She didn't know how long they crawled, squeezed, stooped, and walked through the passages between the castle walls, but it must've been several hours. Her knees and back ached something fierce by the time they reached a metal grate in one of the castle's outer walls.

A sliver of moon hung high in the early afternoon sky, its cycle nearly complete. By her estimation, it was late fall, the breeze through the grate crisp but not freezing. She moved toward the grate, but Eshtak grabbed her arm and held her back.

"Bad men," he whispered. "Dark will hide."

She nodded, but she wanted to keep moving. Sitting idle allowed her mind to dwell on her actions, specifically the ones pertaining to Eshtak. She ruined his life, killed his family and everyone he knew, and yet he came to her rescue.

What kind of a person does that? How can he still call me friend after everything I've put him through?

Emorith tried to find the greater purpose in it, but it eluded her.

Show me Your plan, Ɛätūr.

Time would reveal His plan to her, but she wasn't one of great patience. She wanted to know right then so that she could feel better about herself.

She'd never let herself forget what she did, nor would she forgive herself for it, but perhaps she'd learn to live with it.

If Eshtak can, so can I.

She needed to clear the air, if not for him then for herself. "Eshtak, there's something I need to tell you."

He cocked his head. "Eshtak listens."

"What happened to you... it's my fault." She sat down and leaned against the wall. "Everything's my fault. I'm so sorry. All I could think about was saving Illian."

Eshtak plopped down next to her and took her hand. Tears raced down his cheeks. "Eshtak looked for family, but not see."

"They're gone because of me."

"Not friend's fault. Bad man hates. Eshtak will see family again."

"Don't you understand? They're all dead."

"Not dead. Eshtak feels family. Friend help find?"

"I'm sorry, but..."

How can I tell him there's no hope in saving his family when I still have hope that Illian and Ansgar live?

Emorith squeezed Eshtak's hand. "If it's possible, I'll do everything I can to bring them back."

Eshtak nodded and sniffed.

She wiped her eyes. "Don't you hate me for what I did?"

Eshtak leaned against her side. "Eshtak loves friend. Eshtak forgives."

Emorith sobbed.

How does he love so freely?

† † †

Night fell, but still Emorith and Eshtak waited. Several patrols stalked the night, most likely looking for her, keeping them pinned behind the metal grate. She pondered what she'd do once free from Galondu Castle. The thought of reaching Saskia's and Illian not being there terrified her, but she had faith. If he hadn't made it, at least he wouldn't have suffered like the people of Intus did.

No! Illian is zhiftäd.

She wouldn't allow herself to think otherwise.

Eshtak tapped her on the shoulder. "Eshtak helps friend now."

Emorith rose, moved next to the grate, and peered through the slats. From her vantage point, it looked like the patrols had moved on. "I think you're right. We need to hurry."

Eshtak unlatched the lock at the bottom of the grate and pushed it out. It hinged on the top, so it wouldn't stay open on its own. They'd have to squeeze out the bottom of the opening.

She nudged Eshtak. "You go first."

In a blink, Eshtak slipped out through the bottom of the grate and disappeared. Emorith took a deep breath and pushed the bottom of the grate out. A dozen feet or so separated her from the ground.

I can do this.

She had no choice.

Emorith decided to turn around and exit feet-first so that she'd be able to hang onto the lip before dropping to the ground. It'd make the distance more manageable. Her head slipped underneath the grate before she realized the error in her logic. Nothing else held the grate up, so its full weight crashed down on top of her fingers. Pain splintered through her fingers and hands and up her arms, all the way into her shoulders. She let go of the lip, a scream lodged in her throat and mist in her eyes. Because of the way she let go, she fell backward and not straight down. She braced for impact with the hard ground, but Eshtak caught her in his arms.

As thin and as short as he was, Eshtak possessed unbelievable strength. Emorith thanked him with a nod and climbed out of his arms.

The ring of steel shattered the silence and sent Emorith and Eshtak spinning around. A single soldier cornered them, his sword stretched out in front of him. Eshtak stepped in front of Emorith and pushed her back against the castle wall.

The soldier edged closer. "It's my lucky night."

"Don't count on it." Rage drove Emorith forward, pushing her past Eshtak.

The soldier froze for an instant, obviously stunned by her boldness. She advanced and lunged at him as his sword arced up and back. Armor crunched as she plowed into the center of his breastplate with her shoulder. He fell backward, taking her with him.

By the time they hit the ground, she'd snatched the dagger from his belt and had it arcing downward a second later, only she missed her mark. She'd aimed for his face—or at least where his face should've been—but struck the ground hard instead. The impact jarred the dagger from her grasp, and it clattered out of her reach. It took her a moment to realize that the man didn't move underneath her. Her aim would've been true had the man still had a head. Blood spilled from his open neck and pooled on the ground.

Emorith looked to her right. Red eyes and a large muzzle dripping with blood greeted her. "Raonull." She stood and hugged the beast.

Images flashed in her mind. She whipped around and motioned Eshtak over, but Eshtak just stood there, eyes bulging and mouth gaping. They had no time to waste, so she ran over and shook Eshtak. He blinked several times and stared up at her.

"Are you coming or staying?"

He frowned. "Eshtak stays with friend."

"Come on then, we've gotta get out of here." She turned and rushed back over to Raonull.

Her legs trembled and her knees felt like they'd buckle when she grabbed Raonull's mane.

It's the only way.

Her stomach fluttered. Just like the legends of her childhood, she would become a Rídär Ferzh.

I wonder how long it's been since a wizard or sorceress rode a ferzh?

Emorith pulled herself up onto Raonull's back and then reached back to help Eshtak up.

Eshtak waved his arms and shook his head. "Eshtak run. Eshtak fast."

They didn't have time to argue. "So be it." She leaned forward, grabbed fistfuls of Raonull's mane, and entered his mind with hers. *"Head southwest."*

Raonull jolted forward so fast that Emorith nearly lost her grip. She squeezed his ribs with her knees and ducked her head down to keep the wind from tearing out her eyes. She looked back, expecting Eshtak to be left in the dust, but the little guy kept pace with Raonull, hovering about five feet back. Farther back, the black walls of Galondu Castle continued to shrink. As far as she could tell, no one pursued them.

Raonull veered into the forest where it'd be less likely for anyone to spot them, but it didn't slow him down. Two hours later, Raonull showed no signs of fatigue, though sweat slicked his fur where Emorith sat. However, Eshtak fell farther behind with every minute until she could no longer see him behind them. She leaned in close and urged Raonull to slow down using her mind.

Raonull slowed from a run to a gallop to a trot. About ten minutes later, Eshtak finally caught up, his clothes soaked in sweat. He still managed a smile when Emorith looked over at him.

Just ahead, the forest ended. She entered Raonull's mind once again. *"Let's stop here for a minute."*

Raonull grunted and came to a stop. Emorith slid off his back and held onto his mane until the feeling came back into her legs. Given time, she'd get used to riding him.

If we have the time.

They still had another fifty miles or so to go to reach Diabolus Pes and nothing lay between them and it but fields of grass. A few knolls and glens could provide some cover along the way as well, but much of the terrain stretched flat.

It'd be great if they could rest a few hours before moving on, but their chances of discovery increased tenfold at dawn. They had no choice but to push on, and Emorith needed to convince Eshtak to ride behind her. However, she knew it'd be a hard sell.

Eshtak bent over with his hands on his knees, panting like a dog. Emorith snickered at the irony. "Look, we must make it to Diabolus Pes before dawn. You're gonna run yourself into the ground trying to keep up."

Eshtak stood tall and crossed his arms, but his shaky knees betrayed him. "Eshtak not tired. Eshtak run."

"I know you could—" She took one of his hands. "—but we must reach Illian soon."

He looked over at Raonull and scowled. "Eshtak fears beast. Eats us."

Raonull snorted.

Images of dismembered soldiers swept into Emorith's mind. She turned and glared at Raonull. *"You're not helping,"* she said with her mind.

"I promise I won't let him. He's my friend, just like you are." She smiled. "Friends don't eat friends."

Eshtak huffed, then nodded.

She pulled him up onto Raonull's back. "Hold tight. I wouldn't want to lose you."

Raonull surged forward and into the night.

† † †

The first light of dawn crept up from the west just as they reached the outskirts of Diabolus Pes. Thankfully, Saskia lived on a farm on the north side of town. When they arrived at her property, a young man stood outside with his back to them, tending to some chickens and a few goats.

Emorith would recognize his dark locks in a crowd of a million. She let go and rolled off the side of Raonull before he had a chance to stop. She tumbled several times, got to her feet, and ran toward Illian.

"Illian," she yelled, her chest tight with excitement.

When he turned around, his eyes lit up. "Mother!" He ran to her, and they collided in a big hug that brought them to the ground. She kissed him all over until he finally pushed her away.

Tears streaked down his face. "I didn't think I'd ever see you again."

Eshtak joined the party in the dirt, tackling Illian. "Best friend! Best friend!"

The sentiment of those two words sent pangs of joy rippling through Emorith's body. Saskia came running out of the house, a pitchfork clutched in her right hand and fear in her eyes. She headed straight for Raonull, her fiery red hair waving behind her.

Emorith jumped to her feet and ran to intercept Saskia. "It's okay, Saskia! He's with us."

Either Saskia didn't hear Emorith, or she didn't care. Saskia stopped twenty paces from Raonull and launched the pitchfork at him. It wobbled as it sailed through the air. Raonull snatched it from the air in his massive jaws and snapped the handle into three pieces.

Emorith pulled Saskia into her arms. "It's okay. He's with me."

Saskia pulled away and blinked several times. "Emorith?"

Her red eyebrows slanted toward her slender nose, and her brownish-red eyes glistened in the morning light. Freckles spotted her fair skin in shades of brown and orange. Her beauty hadn't faded one bit.

Emorith lowered her hood. "You miss me?" She took Saskia's hand and squeezed it.

Saskia looked over at Illian, who still lay on the ground with Eshtak. "I… We thought you were dead." She smoothed her red blouse.

Emorith embraced her again. "Nothing could keep me away from Illian." She kissed Saskia's cheek. "Thanks for taking care of him."

Saskia shook her head. "It's the least I could do for an old friend."

"Can we come inside?"

"Yes, yes, of course." She looked over at Raonull. "Except that… thing. Is it what I think it is?"

"A ferzh. His name is Raonull."

"I thought they were legends."

"There's a lot we need to discuss. Magus won't stop until he finds me."

"I know. We made preparations when Illian showed up. He said you'd be a few months behind. We assumed the worst. Thank Ɂäṭūr you're alive."

Ɂäṭūr?

Emorith didn't know Saskia believed in anything.

A greater purpose?

CHAPTER NINE

Emorith smoothed Illian's hair back as she stood on the docks of Cape Timor, the southernmost point of the mainland, with him and Eshtak. She stared into the horizon, as far as her vision would allow, marveling at the sheer distance that the Vastus Ocean stretched. A quiet, desolate world few traveled.

Waves crashed against the rock-lined seaboard walkway, spritzing them with ice-cold water. She'd give anything to stay in that moment with Illian forever, but time didn't favor them. Soon enough, Magus would find her and end her life. Of that, she didn't care, but if he discovered Illian lived, all would be lost.

The last of the sunlight fizzled in the eastern sky. The night approached, far quicker than she'd hoped, infusing the air with a chill that grabbed her bones and shook her core. With the chill came a toxic fear that seeped into her mind.

What if Saskia had betrayed her? Could Magus have charmed Saskia the way he had done her so long ago? Her heart thundered. How well did she really know the woman?

She pulled Illian close as her heart cried out to the God she'd finally come to embrace.

Do what you will with me, but keep him safe, Ȝäţūr.

The simple prayer brought peace to her mind, if only for a moment.

The ocean roared, but its ferocity didn't hide the approaching footsteps to her left. She reached deep within herself and summoned the mezhik she'd relied on for so long, but none came forth. She strained harder, and the collar around her neck turned from a shining silver to a glowing red, but nothing more happened.

Ƹäbräƹär.

How could she have forgotten? Her cheeks burned.

The thought of running tightened her chest. She had few coins to keep Illian, Eshtak, and herself fed and nowhere else to turn, so she must rely on Saskia and her contact—a man whose name she wouldn't disclose—to help them escape from Magus's clutches. Saskia had taken care of Illian for six months, no questions asked. She must trust her.

But I trusted Javana as well.

Emorith turned and faced the approaching figure cloaked in dark-blue robes, pushing Illian behind her. Eshtak hugged her left leg. Her teeth chattered, both from cold and fear. She fought every instinct she'd grown to rely on.

Trust no one. Rely on no one. Fight to survive.

Three rules she'd lived by for so long. Never had she broken two of them at once, let alone all three, but how would she fight without mezhik or her staff?

Illian's hand clung to her cloak and his small frame pressed against her back. She took a deep breath.

Everything for Illian, no matter the cost.

She clenched her jaws and braced herself, but for what she wasn't certain. The tall figure stopped five feet from her, his cloak billowing behind him and his robes pulled taut around the fronts of his legs.

The man lowered his hood. Brown locks slid down the sides of his head and framed his chiseled face. His brown eyes shone in the moonlight, sparkling with flecks of yellow.

The warm smile faded from his face and the left side of his nose rose into a snarl. His left arm shot toward her, his hand outstretched. Tendrils of white light slithered around his fingers—mezhik she'd never seen before.

She jerked back a step, nearly trampling Illian. She pushed him behind her and held her right hand up. "Wait—"

Red eyes rose from the darkness as Raonull barreled toward the man. Strings of saliva hung from his jowls, swinging with each stride.

The man's right arm stretched out to the side, and white light began slithering around his right hand as well.

White lightning shot from the man's fingers and straight at her neck. The jolt caught her breath between lungs and mouth and her eyes mid-blink. She winced, expecting blinding pain to succumb her, but it never came.

Raonull leapt at the man and hit an invisible barrier just inches beyond the man's outstretched hand.

The world refocused as her eyelids slid back up. A glowing, red ring hung in the air between her and the man. Her chest heaved as her hand rose to her throat. Her fingers probed her neck but found neither collar nor laceration.

Tendrils of red light flowed from the glowing collar and into the man's outstretched hand until the red collar faded back to a shiny silver. He clenched his fist and grunted. The collar turned black, then to a grey ash, and then it disintegrated.

Emorith swallowed hard and dipped her head. "Thank you."

Raonull rose from the ground and shook his head. She entered his mind. *"It's okay, my friend. He's here to help."*

Raonull growled and returned to the shadows.

The man's smile returned. "You're welcome, Lady Darkridge."

Lady?

Many terms had been used to describe her, but lady was never one of them. Her cheeks caught fire, and she thanked Ɛäţūr for the concealment of night.

Illian moved underneath her arm, still clutching her cloak. "Have you come to save us?"

The man lowered himself to Illian's height, kneeling on one knee. His smile widened. "A brave warrior like yourself needs no saving. You've rescued your mother already. Are you not here to save us all?"

Pride and love swirled in the pit of Emorith's stomach as Illian released her cloak and took a step toward the man. "Mother said I was brave to go through the mirror, but I didn't feel brave. I wet my trousers."

The man tousled Illian's hair. "Bravery is defined by what you choose to do in the face of fear. You chose to obey your mother, risking death, and you survived. An ounce of bravery like yours could turn the tides of war. I strive to be as brave as you, but my resolve often falters."

The man looked up at Emorith and continued, "That's why I call on those around me to stand against the evils of this world. My bravery isn't built upon the power of my mezhik or the strength of my arms, but by those who choose to stand at my side. Their loyalty to the cause and the daily sacrifices they make to bring peace and honor to Ɂätur and the good people of all Centauria drive me to be bold and brave beyond anything I could ever achieve on my own."

A man of Ɂätur…

He stood and folded his arms. "Some people must be pushed toward bravery and fight against it every step of the way."

His words jabbed her heart deep. How could he know so much about her when she didn't even know his name? As far as she could tell, he wasn't in her head.

Impossible. I'd know.

She wondered how much Saskia had told him. Then again, how much could she have?

She knows nothing of me.

Emorith gasped. The answer stood right next to her.

Illian.

Saskia had six months with her precious son—more than enough time to learn everything about her. None of it mattered though. Time ticked away. Time she couldn't afford to waste.

She reached down and took Illian's hand. Eshtak still clung to her leg. A single thought, and her mezhik stirred within. Rose into her lips. Saturated her tongue. She pushed hard, knowing the man would give in to her persuasive words and the urgency behind them. "Shouldn't we be heading somewhere? I feel we're too exposed standing on this dock."

The man clasped his hands together and nodded. "Yes, of course. We've little time to spare, and I'm droning on." He gestured toward the west. "Right this way. We've got a boat waiting."

Several minutes later, the man led them aboard a narrow sprinter boat. A sparse crew stood on deck: three burly men, and a woman. For some reason she'd hoped one of those men was Ansgar, but her hopes were quickly dashed. She knew better. However, she hadn't expected the woman.

Saskia? What's she doing here?

Illian broke away from Emorith and ran over to Saskia. Eshtak followed him but stopped short and gawked at the small vessel.

Illian jumped into Saskia's arms. "I didn't think I'd see you again!"

Saskia hugged him tight and eyed Emorith. "We might be seeing each other a lot more."

Emorith frowned and moved toward Saskia, but the man caught her arm and pulled her back around to face him. She growled at him, "Release my arm."

He didn't. Instead, he pulled her toward an open door. "We need to talk. *Alone.*"

Had she not used her persuasion? Or perhaps not enough? She dug deep and summoned all that she possessed. "I said, 'Release my arm.'"

"Heard you the first time." He pushed her inside the room and closed the door behind them. "Take a seat."

Emorith huffed and sat down at the small table. A lone candelabrum sat in the middle of the table. Its yellow flame flickered and lit the small room surprisingly well.

She glared up at the man. "You're no different than Magus."

He sat down on the chair across from her. "Why? Because I don't bend to your persuasive words?"

"No, because you don't know how to treat people. You haven't even bothered to tell me your name."

His brow furrowed, and he nodded. "My deepest apologies. I thought Saskia had told you about me." He stretched his arm across the table and held his hand out. "I am Cyrus Nithik."

Cyrus Nithik...

Emorith's eyes grew wide as the name registered in her mind. "You are *the* Cyrus Nithik?" She took his hand. "I've read many books about you. They say that you're one of the most powerful mages in history. Is that true?"

He chuckled and moved his hand. "When you put it like that, it sounds a bit ludicrous."

"I'm sorry. I must sound like a foolish girl."

"It's okay, but we need to move past the pleasantries. I don't want to seem ruder than I already have, but we've little time and you have an important, world-altering decision to make."

World-altering?

"About what?" Her legs trembled underneath the table.

"Pharius is one of the greatest prophets of our time. Are you familiar with him as well?"

A wizard known for his prophetic words.

"Yes, but what does he have to do with this decision I must make?"

"How far will you go to save your son?" he asked.

Emorith grabbed at her chest. "Beyond death. I'd do anything for him."

Cyrus nodded, his face stoic. "Good. What I'm about to ask of you will rip your heart from your chest, but know it must be done. Illian will never be safe here."

Emorith nodded. "I know. Isn't that why we're on this boat? To leave the Ancient Realm?"

Cyrus slid his hand across the table and covered hers with it. "No place on Centauria, no matter how remote, will save Illian from Magus's wrath. Pharius has prophesied about this."

The room blurred. "I don't understand. If he's not safe anywhere, then what choice do I have to make?"

He stared down for several moments and then his gaze met hers. "Have you ever heard of a heart locket?"

Her heart raced. "No."

Cyrus reached inside his robes and pulled out a golden, heart-shaped locket with a golden chain. "Three were forged, but this is the only one that remains in this world." He handed it to her.

She held the locket in the candlelight. The locket—no more than an inch wide or tall, and hardly an eighth-inch thick—rested in her palm. A translucent, red jewel about the size of a large pea adorned the locket's center, and its shape resembled that of an ancient keyhole—a bulbous top attached to a narrow rectangle.

She cocked her head. "What is its purpose?"

"Think of it as a bridge between worlds."

Emorith choked on her own spit and dove straight into a coughing fit. Cyrus rose from his chair and fetched a glass of water from a set of cabinets she hadn't noticed before. He handed her the glass.

She knocked on her chest with her fist, cleared her throat, then emptied the glass. The water soothed her dry throat. She hadn't realized how parched she'd become.

She handed the glass back to Cyrus and leaned back in the chair. "Thank you."

He nodded and set the glass to the side of the table. "As I was saying, you can think of it as a bridge."

She cleared her throat once more as she continued to stare at the locket. "How does this bridge work, and where does it lead?"

"Long ago, mezhik had far greater power than it does today. The mages of old were able to manipulate more than just the four elements of our world. They found a way to bend time and space in a manner that allowed travel between our world and a place they called the Shadow World."

Emorith gazed at the locket harder. It looked no different than other lockets she'd seen before. She looked up at him. "How do you know it works?"

His eyes gleamed, perhaps from nothing more than candlelight, but she thought its source more ethereal. "Because I've been there."

His words were solid. Final. She knew them to be true. Her stomach churned with excitement. "Are you saying that Illian and I can travel to this Shadow World and escape from Magus?"

Cyrus sighed deep and long. The lines in his forehead deepened. "That is one path of the prophecy, but it won't end the way you'd want it to."

"Then what are you trying to say?" She slammed her palm against the table. "From what I know of you, you're not one to mince words or dance around subjects. I am stronger than you think. Just tell me the truth."

He nodded and leaned forward. "There are four paths to this prophecy. The first takes you both to the Shadow World. If you choose that path, you will live in peace for a few years, but Magus will eventually find you there and kill you both. If you both choose to stay here, Magus will hunt you to the ends of the world and you will suffer long before he kills you both. The third path sends you to the Shadow World and leaves Illian here. As with the first, Magus will find you and kill you, but Illian will survive. The last path sends Illian into the Shadow World. This path will save Illian, but your alliances will determine your fate."

"How many years would we have if I choose the first path?"

"Illian's mezhik will never manifest."

"I cannot send Illian into a strange world where he knows no one, so I choose the third path."

"The third path will save Illian from Magus's wrath, but he will still suffer along with the rest of the world. Magus will win the war and cleanse the world of the ʋnzhifțäd and all those who oppose him."

"Then there's no hope?"

Cyrus wagged his finger. "I didn't say that. Choose the fourth path, and we'll have a chance to save the world."

Emorith rose from her chair and stumbled backward. The locket slipped from her hand and fell to the floor. "You want me to abandon my son! How can you ask that of me? Do you not have children of your own?"

Cyrus rose and moved around the table. His gaze met hers. "I do not, nor will I ever. Prophecy has bound me with celibacy."

"Then you know nothing of the pain you're asking me to endure."

"I do know of love, and my heart breaks daily knowing I'll never have the chance to express it."

Emorith turned away and chewed on her nail. "How can I do this?"

"Be brave. Be the hero Illian knows you to be. Redeem yourself for the hand you played in Intus."

She whirled around. "You know of that?"

He rested his hand on her shoulder. "I do, and I understand why you did the things Magus asked of you, but don't let that keep you from doing the right thing now."

Tears streaked her cheeks as Eshtak's face rose in her mind. She destroyed his family and his entire race, yet he still saved her from Magus. She owed hers and Illian's life to him. Neither of them would have survived without his help.

She stared at the locket lying on the floor. "I can't send him alone." Her lips trembled and her voice quavered.

Cyrus reached out and the locket flew into his hand. He stuffed it back into his robes. "He won't be alone."

"Then who?"

He wiped the tears from her cheeks with his thumbs. "Saskia will go with him and get him settled."

"Settled?"

"Yes. I have a friend who lives in the Shadow World. He resides in a desert land they call Arizona. I assure you that Illian will be safe and cared for."

"How can I tell him? How will he understand? He won't want to go."

"I know, and I'd never ask you to use your mezhik on your own son, so let me talk to him."

What choice did she have? She said she'd do anything to save him, and she knew she would. "Will I ever see him again?"

Cyrus wrapped his arms around her and held her tight. "No."

She embraced him, a stranger not an hour before, and wept without restraint. Every moment she'd spent with Illian flashed through her mind, a torrent of images she'd cling to for the rest of her life. Her chest, throat, and jaws ached with agony. Her mind knew the decision had to be made, but her heart begged for another way.

She prayed again to the God she'd cast aside so long ago.

But I know you now, Ƨäʈūr. I beg of you, watch over my son and protect him as your own. Take my life if you must but let him thrive.

She pulled away from Cyrus and sat back down at the table. Her eyes stung with tears, and she did her best to brush them away.

Cyrus crossed over to the set of cabinets and rummaged through them.

"He will live a good life, Emorith. I'm certain of it."

She nodded and fought back the tempest building in her eyes once again.

Cyrus returned to the table and handed her a damp rag. "Clean yourself up. He doesn't need to see you this way."

She knew he was right, but his words still angered her. She held her tongue and placed the rag over her face. Its cold touch dissipated the sting in her eyes and pulled the heat from her cheeks, but it did nothing to soothe her aching heart.

She folded the rag, patted her forehead with it, and set it on the table. A man whose power rivaled that of Magus sat across from her, but Cyrus didn't wield it or flaunt it with pride. Humble and stoic, yet direct and emboldened with passion. Tears glistened in his eyes as well, yet he had no stake in her or Illian's life. His soft gaze left her warm, yet vulnerable.

"And what about Eshtak?" She looked up at the ceiling to keep her eyes from spilling more tears. "After everything I did to him, he still remains loyal to me. He wants to be where I am."

"Eshtak is rare. He has a pure heart and will never abandon a friend, no matter what."

"Can he come with us then?"

"Because of what Magus did to him, he will play a pivotal role in future events. He will stay with us."

"Good." She looked down at her hands folded in her lap. "I think I'm ready." She wasn't, but she never would be.

Cyrus closed his eyes for a moment and then the cabin door opened. Saskia and Illian stepped inside. He motioned them over.

"Is everything okay, Mother?" Illian's voice squeaked.

She wrapped her arms around him and hugged him tight. "I love you to the farthest star and back."

From the day of his birth, she'd always expressed her love for him that way, but never had those words carried more truth than in that moment. Soon, they would be worlds apart, but her memories of him would always be a thought away. She must find solace in that. She had little else.

He pulled back and smiled. "To the ends of the universe."

She kissed his forehead. "Always."

Cyrus cleared his throat. "Illian, there's something your mother and I need you to do."

The boy turned and faced Cyrus. "I know. Aunt Saskia said you have a mission for me and that I must be brave, like Mother."

Cyrus leaned toward Illian and smiled. "She speaks the truth. Did you know that your mother is braver than even I?"

Illian nodded. "The bravest."

"Indeed, but did you know she's a warrior?"

Illian looked back at Emorith, his eyes wide with wonder. He shook his head.

"It's true. Centauria needs her." Cyrus looked at Emorith, his gaze intense. "She is the key to everything. The world will rise or fall by her hand."

Illian clapped his hands together and jumped in the air. "She can do it! She can do anything!"

Cyrus chuckled, but his gaze bore into Emorith. His eyes searched her heart and her soul.

But what will he find in me? Can I be what he demands? What Centauria needs?

She shifted in her chair.

"I know she can," Cyrus said. "She only needs to persuade herself."

Illian settled. "So, what is my mission? Can I be a spy?"

Cyrus slipped from his chair and to one knee. "Your mission is far more important than spying." He grabbed Illian's shoulder and pulled him closer; until his lips nearly met the boy's ear. He whispered, just loud enough for Emorith to catch his words. "You and Saskia will travel to another world where you'll find peace, happiness, and love."

Illian's face scrunched up. "I really wanna see other worlds, but I don't like girls. Can I skip the love part? Maybe find adventure?"

Cyrus chuckled and winked at him. "Trust me, it will be an adventure you'll never forget."

Illian thrust his arm in the air. "I'll do it!" He frowned. "But I'm gonna miss my mother. Will you take care of her while I'm gone?"

"I'll never let her out of my sight."

Illian held up his little finger. "Pinky swear?"

"Better than that. I give you my word, and my word is never broken."

Emorith moved to the edge of her seat and focused on Cyrus's lips, awaiting his next words.

Cyrus's lips never moved again, but his voice filled Emorith's head. *"One day, given that a certain path of prophecy is fulfilled, your great-grandson will return and help save all Centauria."*

Emorith's breath caught in her throat and the cabin spun around her. *Can it be true?*

In spite of the evil she did, could she be redeemed through her son? *Ƨätūr, make it true!*

Cyrus stood and faced Saskia. "Did you retrieve everything I asked you to?"

"Yes. I found all of it where you said it would be."

"Good. Once you arrive, find Gazsi. He's known in the Shadow World as Rico. The maps will lead you to him, and the ring will let him know I sent you."

She bowed and took Illian's hand. "We will not fail."

Cyrus glanced at Emorith. "Say what you must, but hurry."

Emorith sat there on the edge of her seat, but it might as well have been the edge of the world. How does one say goodbye to the only thing they ever did right? She knew he'd live on in her memories to the very end, but would his memories of her remain intact? Would he remember her, truly remember, or would she fade into his past like a spectre in the night?

She crawled on her knees to Illian and embraced him for the final time. Her heart shattered into pieces, but she remained in control of her tears.

Be strong for him. One last time.

"You are the love of my life, Illian."

He hugged her hard. "And you're mine."

She removed the silver bracelet from her right wrist and placed it into Illian's hand. "For good luck, and so you'll never forget me."

He smiled. "I'll keep it safe and give it back to you when I return."

She nodded and kissed his forehead several times. "I know you will." She stood, glared at Cyrus, then left the cabin.

The night surrounded her. Waves crashed all around and rocked the boat with fervor. She stumbled forward and dropped to her knees. She grabbed at her chest, her heart filled with pain.

A bright light flashed behind her, stretching her forlorn shadow across the length of the deck. She knew it wasn't lightning as Illian's presence faded from her mind.

A hand touched her shoulder, and she cowered lower.

"It is done," Cyrus said.

Emorith lifted her gaze to the dark skies and wailed. Lightning streaked across the sky and thunder rumbled behind it, bringing with it a downpour of rain. Within minutes, the rain soaked her to the bone, but she continued to wail.

† † †

Emorith lay on the wooden deck, staring up at the morning sky. Her sorrow had passed with the night, and now a flame of redemption burned in her heart. From that moment forward, she vowed to fight Magus until her last breath.

Illian lived, and she would survive. Nothing else mattered.

But the mirror…

Had Ansgar been the man in that hallway, or had she conjured him out of desperation? Her mind told her that people don't rise from the dead, but her heart insisted he lived.

If you're alive, I'll find you.

She rose from the deck and found Cyrus at the helm. She made her way over to him and stood at his side. "Where are we headed?"

Cyrus smiled, his hair blown back and his robes billowing in the wind. "Toward victory."

DIVE DEEPER INTO CENTAURIA…

Did you enjoy Emorith's story? Explore more of Centauria in Daniel Kuhnley's Epic Dragon Fantasy series, *The Dark Heart Chronicles*. Read *The Dragon's Stone*, book one in the series. Visit danielkuhnley.com for more details.

A wizard told me the stone gives life to the dead.

Could it be real, or was it merely a legend sought after by fools?

Up until that moment, Nardus had no reason to live. A year ago, the love of his life and his three children were murdered in a brutal attack. Even though his flesh still lived, he died with them that fateful day. Now, hope burned within his heart once again.

The wizard claimed many had sought the stone, yet none had returned. But Nardus didn't fear death. He would pay any price to resurrect his family, even if it meant facing otherworldly creatures in a magical trial that no man had ever survived.

It sounded simple enough, but there was a catch: he loathed magic.

So how could he trust this wizard? Out of all the people in Centauria, why did the wizard choose him?

Then again, what difference did it make? What more could he possibly lose?

Nothing.

His name was Nardus, and thus began his quest for the dragon's stone…

The Dragon's Stone is the first book in *The Dark Heart Chronicles* epic dragon fantasy series. If you like vivid new worlds, action-packed adventures, and courageous characters, then you'll love Daniel Kuhnley's ominously imaginative novel.

Buy *The Dragon's Stone* to embark on an epic quest today!

PLEASE TELL OTHERS WHAT YOU THOUGHT

Thank you for taking this journey with me. If you'd like to show your support for my work, please leave a review wherever you purchased this book. It's free to do so, and it'll only take you a minute to write a quick sentence expressing your thoughts about the book.

Your review is especially important to independent, self-published authors like me. Internet and online bookstore algorithms favor books with reviews. They display in search results and at the top of search results more often than books without reviews.

Did you know that there's a minimum number of reviews needed to purchase certain advertising? It's true. Help me reach that threshold by leaving a review. Doing so will help more people find this book and will in turn help me sell more books, which means I can keep authoring more books for you.

Go to danielkuhnley.com/reviews if you need a link to where you can leave a review.

Thank you!

ABOUT THE AUTHOR

Daniel Kuhnley is an American author of Epic Dragon Fantasy, Supernatural Serial Killer, and Christian YA Sci-Fi/Fantasy stories. Some of his novels include *Reborn*, *The Braille Killer*, and *Kiara Kole And The Key Of Truth*. He enjoys watching movies, reading novels, and programming. He lives in Albuquerque, NM with his wife who also writes.

CONNECT WITH DANIEL

danielkuhnley.com/connect